Sunset Tomorrow

E. ERVIN TIBBS

CamCat
Books

CamCat Publishing, LLC
Brentwood, Tennessee 37027
camcatpublishing.com

Hardcover ISBN 9780744302066
Paperback ISBN 9780744301083
Large-Print Paperback ISBN 9780744300475
eBook ISBN 9780744301106
Audiobook ISBN 9780744302400

Library of Congress Control Number: 2020937956

Cover design/book design by Maryann Appel

5 3 1 2 4

For Deanna, whose light pushed back the shadows.

CHAPTER ONE

D awn brought a breaking surf and a thin wash of sunlight that illuminated the beach, transforming it into a lustrous sheet of wet satin, pulled smooth by the retreating tide. In the frothy welter left behind by a departing wave, a waterlogged square of paper swirled to the surface and danced in the backwash like the cape of a matador. Above the surfline, and beyond the water-polished sand, where the waves could no longer reach, a ragged line of flotsam curled like dark lace to the seaward. In the fringe, Jude Tyler sprawled comfortably, his compact body stretched and loose, with a sturdy arm pillowing his head. He lay deep in slumber, unaware that a muse called Fate had just rolled her loaded dice.

The sea pulled back to rally itself for another assault and drew with it the soggy, waltzing note. For a moment the missive lay on the crest, waiting for the wave to gather enough strength to once again assail the shore.

At that moment, stillness came over the sea and time slowed its inexorable march. For a heartbeat, gulls hushed their raucous calls, a distant foghorn held its breath, and the restless mist thickened into a curtain of translucent pearl.

Fate smiled grimly at what she'd wrought, and the wave rolled in, rumbling with determination. That instant of hushed expectation ended, and time's forward rush resumed. A wave, frosted with creamy spume, charged up the beach carrying the small paper rectangle, but exhausted by its invasion, lost momentum and ran out on the beach without enough power to reach the high-mark of the one before.

One small tendril, however, rushed on, carrying Fate's written proclamation. That stream of foam paused, then rushed back to the sea, leaving behind a sodden sheet of paper, lying slack in the curl of Jude's fingers. Faded letters faced the sky with a message that, for this moment, only the gods could read.

And still Jude slept. In repose, his sun-browned face, neither handsome nor ugly, had by virtue of some personal alchemy also managed to escape being ordinary. Clad in ragged shorts, little more than blue-jeans amputated above the knee, he slept easily, his heavy breath disturbing tiny insects that had gathered to feed among the nearby seaweeds and debris.

A thick, red crescent sun pushed above the horizon and began to devour the warm mists that concealed the demarcation between sky and sea. Through a fissure in the mist, a beam of sunlight lanced down and touched Jude's face. He turned his fluttering eyelids away from the light.

He opened his eyes and looked around without a hint of confusion. In late summer, he often slept on the beach, where a cool onshore breeze lessened the effects of a hot summer night. Although he was thirty-three, the rigors of beach life had not yet grown too difficult for him.

It's the parties that sap your strength, he thought. I've got to stay away from the parties. But it was an idle resolution and he knew it.

With the indolence of a sated leopard, he stretched, yawned, and licked his salt-encrusted lips. He started to rise and discovered the piece of paper lying like a dead fish near his hand. Words, painstakingly hand-printed in black ink, drew his gaze as if they possessed the same arresting power of a eulogy chiseled into a headstone. Carefully, he picked up the sheet and spread it across his thigh. Crumple marks had damaged some of the letters, but the text remained legible. It was a poem.

Radiant light came out from me, and in joy I wept.
Now the light is dim, a fading star on a foggy night.

Life once so sweet is now a curse I face with dread.
My courage, carefully hoarded against the gloom,
   is spent.
Oh God, if there be a God, take me instead.

No signature, just a heart-aching cry of pain, written on cheap bond and tossed into the sea. For a long time he stared at the wet scrap, his mind in turmoil. Why did this enigmatic verse bring such a penetrating chill to his soul? It wasn't great poetry, but it had surely been written from the heart, otherwise it would not have so profoundly touched a stranger. And it had touched him, deep where he thought the walls of indifference stood tall enough to protect him.

Oh God, if there be a God, take me instead. How many times had he cried those words?

There had been a time when his life lay before him, a shining pathway that led to the stars and each step took him higher. He'd been joined in the journey by a gentle soul, her smile like sunlight after rain, her eyes as kind and ingenuous as a new-born fawn. Together they were stronger than each one alone, and their ascent swifter.

His mind recoiled from the recollection, for not long after came the Gray Time, a time when life had no love, no music and no laughter. The Gray Time eventually slipped away, but somewhere in its passage, he'd stepped off the rising path to take a way that led down into a shadowy land of indifference. But there he found peace. No one took his measure, and no one tried to cross the dark moat around his heart.

Abruptly, the painful memories became too much to bear. He peeled the poem from his skin and was about to toss it back into the sea, but something made him hang on to it. A tortured soul had composed those words, someone who at this moment knew the same agony he had once endured. It might even be one of his friends. With great care, he folded the note and slipped it into his shirt pocket.

A burst of sunlight warmed him and drove some of the sadness from his heart. Ten years of living in the shadow of grief had taught him how to shed melancholy as if it were a dirty shirt.

He arose and assessed the day. Unlike most Southern California coastal communities, Sunset Beach was usually quiet in the morning. The streets lay empty except for gulls hunting for food among discarded hamburger wrappers.

Threading his way among the dilapidated houses built on the strand, Jude left the beach and made his way toward Pacific Coast Highway. The light was strong now and far to the north, where the vast, sprawling smog machine of Los Angeles had begun to awaken, he saw a thick, brown haze rising to meet the sun.

Crossing the old railroad right-of-way, he came to a narrow street that led past the back door of Old Dan's coffee shop. As he passed through the alley behind the Sittin Pretty hair salon, Lucy, the owner, opened the back door and shook out an apron. Chubby and middle-aged, Lucy had beautiful black eyes and round, red cheeks that would have looked just right on Santa Claus. She gave him a wide smile. "Morning, Jude. You're moving kinda slow today."

"Got nowhere to go, Lucy. And all the time in the world to get there."

She laughed delightedly. "Sometimes, Jude, I can't decide whether you're a simpleton or a Solomon."

"Lucy, do you know anyone who writes poetry—sad poetry?"

A quizzical look wrinkled her smooth brow. "Sorry, Jude."

She turned back into her shop and Jude moved on. Where the alley opened into the side street, a movement caught his eye. The door in a small apartment just ahead opened a crack. Jude smiled. That was Wino Willy's room and he had money again. If Willy was broke, and he usually was, he would have stepped boldly out into the sun.

Although his nickname Wino implied a man of advanced age, Willy had yet to see his thirtieth birthday. Even though he did have an affinity for the jug, he drank no more than anyone else on the beach. Then again, he drank no less either.

Born into a wealthy family and lacking any useful skills, Willy had spent the last three years merely surviving, waiting for an inheritance to work its way through probate. It was a large estate, and many of the young man's relatives were trying to acquire a chunk of it. Once a month, sometimes more often, his lawyer sent him a little money.

Jude ducked behind a dumpster sitting next to Old Dan's restaurant. The door opened no farther, but Jude was patient. The more caution Willy demonstrated, the more money he had, and among Jude's associates, money was considered community property.

Finally, the door swung open, and one pale gray eye peered discreetly around the frame. No one moved. Even the gulls were gone. Willy emerged cautiously, head swiveling and eyes scanning left and right. He was a tall, thin young man with blond hair, bleached white from hours spent in the sun. A bland, vacant expression hid what Jude knew to be a first-rate brain.

Willy at last gave up his circumspection and started toward Old Dan's. When he came abreast of the dumpster, Jude stepped out and laid his arm over Willy's shoulder.

"Willy, my old friend, I'm so glad to see you."

"I don't have any money. I swear I don't."
Willy didn't try to pull away from Jude's
muscular embrace.

"Of course you do, Willy. I can always tell.
You know that."

"Come on, Jude. Give me a break. It's got to
last me all month."

Jude laughed. "But it won't, and you know
that too. You'll get drunk and spend most of
it, then that bunch at the Shack will borrow
the rest."

Willy hung his head, crushed by the truth of
Jude's statement.

He sighed and spoke softly. "Uncle Cragen
says I don't have proper respect for money.
Guess he's right."

"Forget it," said Jude. "Your Uncle Cragen
is a jerk. If he gave a church the same devotion
he gives his bank account, he'd be a saint." He
shook Willy in a friendly way. "Look, why don't
you loan me twenty? Then you can tell the
borrowers I got it all. At least I pay you back."

Willy sighed, extracted a thin fold of bills,
and peeled off a twenty for Jude.

"Come on," said Jude. "Cheer up. We'll eat breakfast, then we'll go down to the Shack and have a beer."

A solid grunt came from inside the dumpster, and someone cleared his throat.

"Eatin' breakfast is stupid. Maybe we drink breakfast instead."

Jude lifted the edge of the dumpster's lid. "Come on out, Sherm."

A head appeared slowly, like the upthrusting of a toadstool through sod. Sherman's bright, close-set eyes shone with anticipation, and wilted cabbage dripped from his splayed beard. He sat up and shook his powerful shoulders like a wet mastiff, spraying vegetable scraps and damp paper. Jude noticed the scar on the side of Sherman's head was now hidden by thick black hair.

"Willy got money?" Sherman licked his lips.

Jude decided to try a diversion. "Where are Crazy Ed and Lonesome?"

Sherman shrugged and hauled himself out of the dumpster.

"Went to a party last night. Haven't seem 'em since."

Reaching back into the dumpster, Sherman withdrew a gallon bottle with a hand's breadth of Red River wine remaining. Triumphantly, he raised it, resembling a barbarian holding a giant ruby up to the sun.

"Where did you get that?" asked Jude. Sherman never had money.

Sherman furrowed his brow and pursed his lips. He shrugged. "Can't remember."

"Don't matter," said Willy. "Give me a drink."

Sherman's blank expression turned to cunning. "You loan me enough for nuther bottle?"

"Yeah. Now give me a drink."

After the bottle had made another round, the three seated themselves on the guardrail along a curve on the Pacific Coast Highway. For a while, they sat in comfortable silence, watching traffic.

The pleasant quiet was broken by a distant voice. "Hey, guys."

"Here come Lonesome," said Sherman, without looking around.

Jude peered over his shoulder to see the tall young woman bearing down on them with the gait of a racing thoroughbred. Long hair, the color of spun caramel, had been pulled back in a ponytail that waltzed around her slender neck as she moved. Over her shoulder, she carried a shovel.

She stopped and sat down next to Sherman. When her panting breath diminished, she grabbed the bottle, drank deeply, and returned the empty to a scowling Sherman.

"What's the shovel for?" asked Jude. "You going to do some work?"

Lonesome crinkled up her dark blue eyes, compacting the freckles across her nose into a brown haze. "You crazy?"

"Why are you carrying a shovel then?"

She frowned at the shovel as if she'd just realized it was a tool. "There's going to be a minus tide in about an hour."

Willy sat up quickly. "You sure?"

Minus tide meant there were clams to dig and the possibility his money wouldn't be spent on food.

"Damn straight," said Lonesome. "I just looked at Vinny's tide book. We got about an hour."

"That shovel won't work for digging clams in the surf," said Jude. "We need to find Vinny's pitchfork."

"And more wine," said Sherm.

As they rose to leave, a sound stopped them—a rhythmic, ear-piercing squeak coming from a nearby alley. "I think we're about to be ambushed by Cowboy Toby," said Jude.

A small boy emerged from the shadows riding a two-wheeled tricycle. Cowboy Toby had acquired his strange vehicle because someone had found the old tricycle in a trash bin and passed it on to the little boy. His mother worked as a waitress and made just enough money to keep them both from starving. There was seldom anything left to buy toys. Its wheel bearings had long ago rusted away, and when he rode, the noise could be heard for blocks. Just before his fourth birthday, one rear wheel had collapsed and fallen off, but the loss didn't bother Toby.

He'd adapted and learned to ride it balanced precariously on two. It was an extraordinary sight.

When the wheel failed, Jude had offered to replace it, but Toby, with a shy smile, declined.

"It's almost like a bicycle," he said.

Toby stopped and used one leg to balance himself astride his lopsided steed while he straightened his white cowboy hat. He had spent most of his years in hospitals fighting a rare degenerative cancer. His hat concealed a head stripped clean of hair by chemical therapy.

"You guys going to the Shack?" he asked.

"Yup," said Jude. "That where you're headed, little pardner?"

Another shy smile warmed the boy's face. "I'm sposed to warn Crazy Ed if I see you coming."

"Well, you better get over there and do that, Scout," said Jude.

"Naw," said Toby. "I told him I wouldn't spy on you."

The boy's adoration made Jude uncomfortable, and he changed the subject.

"Why don't you let me squirt some oil on those wheels so they don't squeak so loud?"

The little boy's face lit up. "Don't matter. Tomorrow's my birthday, and Mama's going to buy me a real bike. We already went to the hardware and looked at it. It's blue, just like the ocean." His eyes glowed with anticipation.

"How old you going to be tomorrow?" asked Lonesome.

Toby studied a moment, then held up a hand with all fingers and a thumb extended from the other. "Six." He hitched up his drooping pants. "Soon when I get a real bicycle, I'm going to run errands for mom cause she's so tired all the time."

"That's a real good thing," said Jude.

"Got to go," said Toby. With the careless grace of a circus acrobat, he balanced his odd little vehicle and turned back into the alley. "Mom's fixin' breakfast."

He rode away, squeaking and waving.

An odd feeling came over Jude. A mix of compassion and respect. "I wish I was as brave as that little boy."

Only Lonesome heard, and she gave him a strange look.

Sherman broke the silence. "We know Crazy Ed is at the Shack." He gave Jude a sly look. "And he don't want us to know he's there."

"That's because he's got money." Lonesome said the words incredulously as if she had caught herself lying.

Willy looked dubious. "Where the hell did Crazy Ed get money?"

"Some tourist got drunk at the Shack last night and loaned it to him."

"Damn! That inlander must have been sloshed out of his mind."

"Her mind," corrected Lonesome.

Sherman looked as reverent as a country preacher. "Everybody got money," he said. The reverence mutated slowly to anticipation and cunning. "Now we have a party."

CHAPTER TWO

Hazy sunshine saturated the air without warming it, and a cool breeze, effervescent as dry champagne, blew in from the sea.

Jude breathed in huge gulps of the pungent air, savoring the rich taste and aroma, ultimately more intoxicating than any wine.

Although this fine summer morning held great promise of charm and leisure, it refused to nourish any sense of urgency. He and his friends walked slowly and in companionable silence as they made their way to the Shack.

To Jude, and to the others in lesser degrees, each sunlit moment was a treasure to be hoarded, relished until its taste, smell, and touch were utterly exhausted, then grudgingly released. Without any grand philosophical reflection, they chose to measure their existence in that fleeting, ephemeral instant known as the present.

~❦~

The Shack was more of a description than a name. Built on skids, the little clapboard building had survived the 1933 Long Beach earthquake. The original brick red exterior faded long ago to the color of cedar bark, and its white trim darkened with mildew. The entire building seemed to be bent on reaching color equilibrium with the surrounding beach.

A painted wooden sign had once graced the facade, but it had warped and fallen and was later burned by a passing tourist to cook clams. Few could remember the original name, and no one cared. One-legged Vinny had owned the little beer bar for as long as the residents of Sunset Beach could remember. He called it The Shack, and that was good enough for the patrons.

Just outside the door, Jude stopped. "If Crazy Ed's got money, he'll be harder to pin down than a jelly fish at high tide."

"Yeah, and he can run like a scalded cat," said Willy.

"We'll surround him," said Jude. "Sherm, you and Lonesome go around to the back door. Me and Willy will go in the front."

He got a sly grin from Lonesome. "Good thinking, Jude. You should be a general."

She and Sherm made their way around the building.

When he was sure his troops were in place, Jude led Willy through the door. The Shack's interior was no more remarkable than the outside. It consisted of a square room with a three-sided bar taking up about half the floor space. Between the two ends of the bar sat an old brass cash register, and next to it, with his chair leaned back against the wall, lounged One-legged Vinny reading a newspaper.

Across the room, near the only window, sat a rickety table surrounded by benches and one crippled rocking chair. Faded photographs of forgotten people and momentous events shared the walls with dingy posters, all coated with a dark brown patina of old tobacco smoke.

Stepping into the somber light, Jude stopped. He caught the quick movement of a shadowy figure ducking behind the far side of the bar. And where the shape had disappeared, a half empty mug of beer, foam still running down its side, sat abandoned. Nearby, an old man stared at the mug as if he'd just witnessed an act of magic.

Chuckling, Jude straddled the nearest stool. "Somebody must have told us a wild story, Willy. Crazy Ed hasn't been here. He would never leave a half glass of beer."

Leaning against the bar beside him, Willy grinned. "You're right, Jude. Ed's got more class than that."

The old man shook his head slowly. "I was talking to him, and he just goddamn disappeared," he muttered. He drank the last of his beer and shuffled out through the front door.

One-Legged Vinny peered over the top of his newspaper. "You got money?"

"We do." Jude pointed to Willy.

Vinny waved his hand toward the beer taps. "Help yourself."

Snagging two mugs from behind the bar, Jude leaned over to fill them from a spigot. He set one in front of Willy. The other he drained without setting it down and quickly refilled.

"Willy, put some money on the bar," he said.

With a kick, Vinny rocked his chair upright. He grabbed his crutch and heaved himself erect, leaning heavily on the structure of yellow wood, permanently bowed by his enormous weight. Vinny owned a prosthetic leg but refused to wear it.

"You guys keep track of how many you drink. I'm going out back." He made his way through the rear door and across a narrow alley, where an out-building housed the restroom.

Jude nudged Willy and whispered. "Follow my lead."

Willy nodded.

"Out on the street, Willy." Jude let his voice rise excitedly. "Look! That girl's bikini is smaller than an eyepatch."

"Man," said Willy. "It doesn't cover anything."

Although their remarks seemed to indicate their attention was directed elsewhere, neither Jude nor Willy moved their eyes from the dripping mug. While they watched, a hand crawled into view, wrapped around the glass, and without spilling a drop, slid it gently over the edge. The glass reappeared, empty.

With a quick scuffling sound, a shadow ducked out the back door. Jude and Willy touched glasses and drank deeply.

Wiping foam from his lip, Willy peered out the back door. "Crazy Ed's moving fast. He must not be drunk yet."

Jude nodded sagely. "Probably has some money left too."

From outside came a sharp yelp of surprise. A few seconds passed, and Crazy Ed stumbled back through the door, Sherm holding one arm with Lonesome on the other.

"He try to run," said Sherm.

"I tackled him in the alley," Lonesome added.

With an impatient swipe, Ed brushed sand from his long black hair. "How did you guys know I got money?"

"Word gets around," explained Jude.

A look of defeat crossed Ed's long face. "You're a goddamn mind reader." He put a crumpled bill on the bar and helped himself to a pitcher and two glasses.

"We're going clam digging," said Jude. "Know where we can find Vinny's clam fork?"

Crazy Ed shook his head. "Haven't seen it since last low tide." He poured beer for Sherm and Lonesome.

Vinny thumped through the back door, drying his hands.

"You guys left it in the alley. Some tourist probably stole it."

"Maybe we can borrow one from the baitshop," Lonesome offered. The eternal optimist, she knew but refused to accept the universal animosity of Hal, the baitshop owner, toward all those who did not work for their living.

"Hal wouldn't loan us a gutter to die in," said Ed.

"Maybe he don't need to know we borrowed it," offered Willy.

"No," said Jude. "Hal watches us too closely, and there's no time to plan a diversion."

Leaning over the bar, Vinny peered at Sherm. "What the hell's wrong with Sherm? He looks constipated."

"He's thinking," said Jude.

Vinny leaned closer. "Damn! I never seen him do that before. You sure?"

"Yup. Seen him do it once about a month ago."

"When he tricked the tourist into buying him a jug of Red River?"

"That's it."

Lonesome took Sherman's arm. "Sherm, stop that. You're going to hurt yourself."

The big man ignored them. "We need — clam fork," he finally got out.

"Okay." Lonesome sounded agreeable. "We know that, but you let Jude do the thinking. That's what he does best."

"What do you need a clam fork for?" The voice was feminine and unfamiliar.

Two well-dressed women had slipped unnoticed into the bar. One was having trouble getting onto the barstool. She looked drunk.

Jude classified them instantly. Female. Wealthy. Bored. Their type appeared frequently on the beach; middle aged, often full of booze, and desperately trying to recapture their youth. The women were more welcome than the men. They rarely wanted to fight and usually had more money to spend.

"Conditions are good for digging clams." Jude added his friendliest smile.

"Oh!" said the drunk one. "Never dug clams before."

The sober one, an attractive lady of perhaps fifty with eyes a bit too hard, gave Jude a long appraising look, then held out her hand.

"My name is Ellen. Tell me more about clam digging."

With a sigh of relief, Jude leaned over and patted Sherm's shoulder. "You can quit thinking now."

The strained expression disappeared from Sherm's broad face. He downed a full glass of beer. "Thinkin' make me thirsty."

Grabbing the pitcher, Lonesome refilled his glass. "Everything makes you thirsty."

Jude turned back to the two women.

"There's a big sand bar about sixty feet offshore. If the tide is low enough, you can dig clams there; big Pismo's the size of hubcaps. They make the best clam chowder in the world." He sighed despondently. "But we don't have a clam fork."

"Where can I get one?" asked Ellen.

"Hal's Bait Shop, just down the street."

She turned to her friend. "What do you think, Marge?"

Marge shrugged. "Beats the hell out of playing bridge with that pack of bitches at the Yacht Club."

"Okay. You come with me, Marge. If I leave you here alone, you might steal this handsome young man."

Marge leered at Jude and fell off her stool. Ellen helped her up and led her out the door.

When the two women were safely out of earshot, Willy spoke. "Those two inlanders will just get in the way. The water's going to be cold, and I want to get in and out quick as possible."

"Me too," said Jude. "We'll just have to think of something."

Before they could agree on a strategy, the women returned carrying a clam fork with a price tag still fluttering from the handle.

"We're ready now," said Ellen. Marge leaned against the bar, futilely trying to swing her leg over a stool.

"Did you get a knife?" asked Jude.

Abruptly, Marge stopped trying to mount the stool and managed to focus on Jude. "Why the hell would we need a knife?"

"You didn't tell them?" Lonesome's voice squeaked with alarm.

The room fell silent as if everyone was reluctant to discuss some special horror. Jude let the silence draw out.

"The giant killer clam," he said softly, letting a degree of awe creep into his voice.

Ellen laughed. "You're putting us on."

"They all say that at first, lady." Jude drew a long face. "Truth is, the giant killer clam got my best friend."

"How did a giant clam get in these waters?" asked Ellen. "They're a tropical species."

Jude hadn't counted on zoological knowledge.

"In the hold of a banana boat," said Willy. "It was little then. Got pumped out with the bilge water."

Vinny choked and coughed while turning away to wash glasses.

Lifting his glass, Crazy Ed managed to look teary-eyed. "A toast to old George. He was a hell of a man. Fought that clam right down to the end."

"But we never saw him again," said Willy.

"At least not in one piece," Ed added.

Mournfully, Jude shook his head. "Every few days, a bone would wash up on the beach. Took us six months to collect enough to bury."

"Never did get his left foot," said Lonesome.

"To hell with it," said Marge. She gave up trying to mount the stool and leaned against the bar. "Water's probably cold anyway."

Ellen held up her clam fork. "You mean, I bought this thing for nothing?"

"Why don't you let me borrow it?" Jude patted her on the shoulder. "I'll bring you some clams."

She looked suspicious. "You're not afraid of the Giant Killer Clam?"

"I got a knife," he said. "And I'm anxious to avenge old Gregory."

"I thought his name was George."

"Yeah," said Jude. "Old George Gregory. Hell of a man."

CHAPTER THREE

J ude paused as he reached where the beach steepened and led down to the retreating surf. His friends gathered around him. Although the sun was well up, sustaining the promise of a warm day, the breakers looked cold, gray, and hard as lead.

The sea, the mother of life, but she cared little for her children, thought Jude.

Last night, someone had tossed a poem into those pitiless waves, an act of utter despair.

"Willy, you ever write any poetry?"

Willy stared as if he'd misunderstood. "Poetry. What the hell you talking about?"

"Just a thought," said Jude. A rush of foam writhed around his toes, and the chill caused him to shiver.

"Water's cold," said Willy. "Wish we could wait till the sun was higher."

"Tide won't wait," Jude replied.

Crazy Ed stepped up to the surf line. "Come on, Sherm. Let's get this over with."

Jude waded the surf until the water swirled around his calves. Out beyond the breakers, he could see the smooth rushing of water over the sand bar. He hoped the tide was low enough to permit them to stand. Free diving for clams was hard, cold work, made especially so because none of them owned a wet suit.

With a shout, Willy ran toward the incoming breaker and dove into the foaming precipice. Jude tightened his grip on the clam fork and followed. After him came Lonesome, swimming side-stroke and holding a wine bottle above the water with her free hand.

Behind Lonesome, Sherman crashed through the first wave, saltwater dripping from his curly hair like rain from a black cloud. He swam with short, powerful strokes while Crazy Ed hung onto his belt with one hand and a burlap bag for collecting clams with the other. Ed had never learned to swim, so he relied on Sherman's strength to drag him across sixty feet of deep water.

On reaching the sandbar, Willy stood up, and in the trough between waves, the water reached his waist. Jude joined him and shivered as he shook seawater from his hair.

"Looks like we'll be diving today."

"Yeah," said Willy. "Must have missed the lowest point of the tide."

Arriving last, Lonesome uncorked the bottle and passed it around. Taller than all the men except Ed and having longer arms, she could keep the bottle above the breakers. And, as Keeper of the Wine, she was exempt from actually having to grub for clams.

Jude handed the fork to Ed. "You dig, and the rest of us'll take turns diving."

Ed began to shove the fork into the sand, moving slowly with his back to the waves. Almost immediately, the fork grated against something solid.

"It's a big one," he said.

"I'll get it." Jude took a deep breath and flipped head first into the cold, foamy water. It closed around him, frothing and bubbling as he pulled himself to the bottom with the fork's wooden handle. He felt Sherm's beefy hand around his ankle. Sherman held to a rigid clam digging philosophy. If you didn't get the clam, you didn't come up for air.

Jude jammed his hand into the sand around the tines and felt the rough oval shell. It was a big one. He loosened it and held it out of the water. Sherm wouldn't release his foot until the big man saw the clam.

Jude surfaced and wiped the water from his face.

Sherman's eyes were bright with anticipation. "We eat it now?"

"No," said Jude. "This water's too damn cold to stay in very long. We eat when we get to shore."

"Okay," said Sherman. "Me next."

An hour later, they came out of the surf shivering and dragging a heavily laden bag. The wine bottle was empty and the bright early morning sunlight didn't provide enough warmth to drive away the chill. They ran for the Shack.

Inside, they found Vinny waiting with a crock-pot full of hot red wine. Grinning widely, he poured each one a steaming mug.

Jude took a big gulp. Slowly—with great care—he set the mug on the bar. Searing liquid slammed into his stomach like molten steel; hot vapors rushed up and lifted to the top of his head. He gasped and looked around. The rest of his group stood slack jawed and stunned.

Lonesome took a breath. "Whew!"

A chuckle rumbled from Vinny's immense belly. "Put a little brandy in it. Thought you'd appreciate that."

"How much is a little?" Willy's voice sounded cracked and wheezy.

"Whatever was left in the bottle." Vinny poured himself a mug and drank as if it were iced tea.

"How big was the bottle?" Jude sniffed the mug, and his sinuses opened.

A sly grin twisted upon Vinny's massive face. "About a gallon."

Jude cleared his throat.

"I don't feel cold anymore." The rest nodded their agreement and sipped their incendiary concoction silently.

He surveyed the bar. "Where did the two women go?"

With a casual gesture toward the door, Vinny turned away and began to refill the crock-pot.

"Went to get the makins for clam chowder. I told 'em what to buy."

"Hallelujah," said Crazy Ed. "Now we'll eat like kings."

Willy offered a sour look. "Something bad will happen. It always does."

"What the hell are you talking about?" Crazy Ed replied.

"Stop and think," said Willy. "A couple a years ago we made a big pot of chowder, and it tipped over. Scalded that old tomcat that lives under the Shack."

"Oh bullshit, Willy," said Jude. "That goddamn cat lost a little hair off his ass. It didn't even stop him from eating the clams."

Mournfully Willy shook his head, held up his hand and began to tick off fingers.

"Last year, Lonesome broke her arm the day after we made chowder. When we did the same thing a couple a months ago," he paused for dramatic effect, "I got sick and had to go to the emergency ward."

"You got sick cause you tried to chug-a-lug a gallon of Red River."

Willy looked stubborn.

"We should just boil them clams and eat. Chowder is bad mojo, and something real bad is going to happen."

"Hold it," said Jude. "Everybody who wants chowder, hold up their hand."

All hands went up except Willy's.

"You're outvoted," said Jude.

"Bad mojo," muttered Willy.

Jude heard the door open behind him. In the mirror over the cash register, he saw the figure of a man hesitate, looking for empty space at the bar. With heavy-footed steps, he made his way to the far side and slid onto a stool.

He was a big man by any measure, but age and self-indulgence had rounded the edges and softened the corners. On his square, blunt face, a trace of character remained but so slackened and eroded, it created no lasting impression.

Wide shoulder pads inserted in his expensive jacket allowed it to drape properly over his growing paunch. His left hand sported a pinkie ring set with a ruby and only slightly smaller than his knuckle. Peeling a twenty from a gold money clip, he flipped it negligently on the bar.

"Set up the house and bring me a bottle of Bud."

"Everybody is drinking hot wine," said Vinny. "But I'm sure they wouldn't turn down a beer for later."

The man waved dismissively.

"Whatever they want."

Vinny drew beer for the regulars and returned with the man's Budweiser.

"You own this place?" asked the man.

"I own the business," said Vinny. "The property comes with a hundred-year lease."

"So I've heard," said the man. "You must be Vinny." He extended his hand. "Dirk Bouchard."

Vinny took Dirk's hand with a wary look.

"You interested in selling this," Dirk gazed around the room condescendingly, "business."

"Nope," said Vinny. "Think I'll just hang in there."

"Times are changing," said Dirk. "There's people beginning to look at all this beach property and see its possibilities."

"Are you one of those people?" asked Jude.

Dirk gave him a bland look. "I don't think I know you."

"I know damned well you don't. But I know you. You're the rich guy building a new house in Surfside."

A smile thinned Dirk's full lips. "You make it sound like an accusation."

"I have a suspicious mind," said Jude. "Especially when an old lady's home burns to the ground and before the smoke clears, someone buys the lot."

Dirk's smile disappeared. "Are you accusing me of something specific." His voice had a crack of authority now.

"Of course not," said Jude. "That could be construed as slander, and even this poor ole beach bum ain't that stupid."

For a while Dirk studied Jude. "I can't seem to get a handle on you. You look like a derelict, but obviously you're a clever fellow."

"The name is Jude."

"Well, Jude, let me give you some advice. If you want something you've got to reach out and take it. It's pretty obvious you haven't done that."

"While we're handing out advice," said Jude, "let me pass on some of my own. Fires tend to get out of control. You just never know what might burn next."

"I don't like being threatened by a bunch of alcoholics," said Dirk.

Jude laughed, a sound that conveyed little humor. "We aren't alcoholics, just common everyday drunks. But what you like or don't like isn't even on our list of priorities."

Dirk gave him another smile, this one tinged with respect.

"You got brass balls, son. Big ones, that probably clank when you walk."

Deliberately, Dirk picked up his change, folded the bills, and replaced them in his money clip.

He left the coins.

Taking a card from his inner pocket, he placed it on the bar.

"I have a feeling you're a man who's a hell of a poker player but too smart to play games of chance." He finished his beer and stood up. "If you ever think about legitimate work, give me a call. I'm always on the lookout for men who are smart and tough."

At the door, Dirk turned and spoke to Vinny. "Think about selling. I might make you a really good offer."

Vinny nodded but said nothing. When Dirk was gone, Vinny refilled Jude's glass. A wide grin creased his face. "If I saw a squadron of flying pigs pass overhead, it would surprise me less than if you went to work for a man like that."

"To hell with him," said Jude. "Let's make some clam chowder."

Vinny refilled all the beer mugs. "Guess you guys better start looking for firewood." He pointed at Sherman. "And if you burn my toilet door again, I'm goin' to make you pay your tab."

"Okay," said Sherman.

"Where's the kettle?" asked Jude.

"Out by the barbecue."

Vinny owned a small dilapidated motel next door, and in the center of the courtyard stood a fire-blackened ring of bricks. Originally, it had been built as a planter, but Vinny was legendary for two attributes; his enormous capacity for beer and his total lack of horticultural skills. Several generations of begonias, snapdragons, and roses had been planted, watered, and carefully tended to only to wilt and die—some overnight.

The old timers claimed Vinny persisted for five years before finally concluding that cultured flowers were not to his liking anyway. He decided to let grow and nourish whatever weeds could be induced to call his planter home. The following spring, a small dandelion sprouted its thin anemic stalk, supporting one tender leaf.

For a time, it looked hopeful, but in the span of one weekend, it shriveled, curled, and quietly succumbed. After that, Vinny conceded defeat, and the planter became the community outdoor barbecue.

Today, a huge, round kettle sat next to the fire ring. Jude inspected it and found it clean enough not to worry too much about food poisoning.

"Sherm, you, Lonesome, and Ed find some firewood. Willy, you get some fresh water, and I'll clean the clams."

When the scavengers returned, Crazy Ed and Lonesome carried great armloads of driftwood; most of it dry. Sherman's contribution consisted of a stack of boards that looked suspiciously like house siding and a wooden toilet seat.

"Is that toilet seat from the Shack?" asked Jude.

Sherm looked innocent. "Nope."

"Better burn it first," said Willy, "in case someone comes looking."

While Jude arranged the wood in the barbecue, he heard the sound of Cowboy Toby's tricycle. The little boy wheeled around a corner, pedaling furiously, a paper bag hanging from one hand.

He brought his trike to a halt next to Jude, dismounted, and held out the bag.

"It's the salt and pepper from the Shack," he said. "Mama borrowed it from Vinny, but she said you'd need it for the clam chowder."

"Thanks little pardner," said Jude. "You going to stay and eat with us?"

Toby shook his head vigorously. "Can't. Mama's takin' me to the doctor today." He stuck his hands in his pockets and scuffed the sand with his toe. "Mama said I shouldn't bother you . . ."

"You can bother me any time you want."

"I never rode a bicycle before," Toby said softly.

"Nothing to it," said Jude. "It'll probably be easier than riding your old trike, but I'll be glad to help you learn."

"Wow, thanks." Toby's eyes shone with anticipation. "Mom said to come right back." He remounted his trike and started across the courtyard.

"You be careful, and don't break the sound barrier," Jude called after him. "You know how that upsets your mother."

Toby looked over his shoulder and grinned, his eyes sparkling with humor. "Sometimes, Jude, you are so silly."

Jude flinched as if he'd been struck. Almost word for word, Toby had spoken a line used often and with great affection by someone who, long ago, had loved him without reservation. Those innocently spoken words opened a portal into his past, and a suppressed memory escaped from its dark prison. As always, the memory brought with it a monster—pain—a deep, smothering ache that crept out of his soul and lay siege to his heart. It was a grief he'd battled to vanquish for over a decade . . . unsuccessfully. With horrible effort, he thrashed the demon back into the hidden depths of his being and slammed shut the iron gate that closed it off from his heart.

To hide his distress, he carefully lit the fire.

The others joined him, and together they lifted the pot of water and placed it over the fire.

"Smells good," said Sherm.

"That's crazy," Lonesome expressed. "The water isn't even hot yet."

Sherm licked his lips. "Smell good anyway."

As they waited for the water to boil, an old, gray Volkswagen pulled out of the side street and onto Pacific Coast Highway.

"Isn't that Shelly, Toby's mother?" asked Lonesome.

"Yes," said Jude. "She's taking him to the doctor."

As the old car wheezed closer, the passenger side window rolled down, and Cowboy Toby leaned out. He waved, a little boy wave, using only his fingers.

When the car had disappeared into the distance, Jude turned to his friends and found them immersed in an odd silence. There was a look in Lonesome's eye he'd never seen before.

The pot was simmering when the two women returned with a large bag of potatoes, a small one of onions, and a couple of large jugs of milk. Marge had sobered up a bit and helped Lonesome and Willy peel and chop the potatoes.

Ellen sat beside Jude and watched while Crazy Ed fished clam shells out of the pot with a tire iron. "Your friends are a little bit careless about cooking hygiene," she said.

Jude held up a bottle of Red River.

"If cheap wine doesn't kill you, what chance has food poisoning?"

She chuckled lightly.

"All of you seem to be a hardy lot. The big fellow with the beard looks like a weight lifter."

"Not Sherm," said Jude. "He never lifts anything heavier than a can of beer."

"He seems to have a speech impediment."

"A chunk of his brain is missing."

"Oh dear." She looked genuinely embarrassed. "I didn't mean to sound pompous."

"Forget it," said Jude. He passed her the wine bottle. "Sherm's learned to live with it."

She drank and returned the bottle. "God!" A coughing fit seized her, and between gasps, she took a deep breath. "That stuff is horrible." She watched Sherman break a heavy board in his bare hands. "How did it happen—his injury I mean?"

"Until a few years ago, he was a foreman in a Michigan steel mill. A careless crane operator dumped a full load of half inch rebar on the work floor. When it hit the concrete, it bounced and exploded in every direction. Sherm yanked a couple of guys out of the way. They weren't hurt, but Sherman took a piece through his skull. Part of his speech center's missing."

Ellen took the wine bottle from Jude and drank again.

"Sad," she said. "Will he ever be . . . normal?"

"Two years ago, he couldn't put three words together in a row. Lonesome says when she first met him, he could barely speak."

"Lonesome is his girlfriend?"

"They're friends. She was on her way to California after a nasty divorce. Sherm was hitchhiking, and she picked him up. They live in a little room across the highway."

"They are lovers then?"

"Don't know," said Jude. "Never asked. Sherm has a hole in his head, and Lonesome has a hole in her heart. Guess they complement each other."

She gave him a strange look and sighed. "Do you have a girlfriend?"

"I have a lot of friends, some of the feminine gender."

Again, she gave him a strange look. "You are aware, I suppose, that one minute you sound like an amiable idiot and the next a college professor."

Jude squinted at the sun. "Maybe there's just not that much difference between the two."

She leaned back and studied him. "In spite of your bravado, I sense a good, thoughtful mind. Do you have any college?"

"Just enough. I learned that twenty thousand years ago mankind domesticated the dog, about five thousand years ago, he discovered beer, and that not much of importance has happened since."

Her expression became vaguely sad. "Do you ever take anything seriously?"

With a wave of his hand indicating everything around him, Jude said, "Sunshine, wine, the deep brine, and beautiful women — in whatever order they appear, and as long as I can have them all."

The roar of a powerful motorcycle interrupted them. The sound stuttered and slowed, and out on the street, a bike and rider came into view, rolling to a slow stop. Although the motorcycle was huge, the rider dwarfed it. His black leather jacket was scarred and battered, his hat was a shapeless mass of crushed felt, shadowing close-set blue eyes. A massive red beard touched with gray fell to his waist where it met a length of chain that secured his faded blue jeans.

The rider raised his head and sniffed the air.

Again, the engine roared and the big, black bike rolled slowly into the courtyard. Ellen gasped, and her face paled. Holding his wine bottle, Jude rose to his feet. He sensed his comrades gathering behind him. The bike stopped inches from his legs. He and the bearded leviathan stared at each other for a long heartbeat. The rider spoke in a voice that sounded like a rock crusher. "That smells like clams cooking."

"It is," said Jude.

The rider grinned, exposing yellow teeth. "What would I have to do to get some?"

"Easy," said Jude. "Bring a jug of wine or a case of beer, and you'll be a lifelong friend."

The big man laughed. "And if I bring both?"

"You'll be nominated for godhood."

"Where's the nearest liquor store?"

"Across the highway."

The big man nodded and started to turn the bike. Jude held out the wine bottle. "One for the road?"

The big man took the bottle and saluted Jude. "My friends call me Heavy." He drank deeply, smacked his lips with satisfaction, and returned the bottle. "Be right back."

True to his word, Heavy returned carrying three cases of beer and two jugs of Red River. He was received and hailed in a manner that would have gratified a conquering Caesar on his return to Rome.

The boiling liquid began to thicken, and Jude added spices: a half handful of salt, a handful of black pepper, and one small bottle of hot sauce. In spite of its simplicity and the crude culinary methods used to prepare it, the aroma was of ambrosia.

Jude took Sherm's arm. "You guard the pot. Don't let anyone start eating until the clams stop moving."

Before long, even Sherm's ominous presence wasn't enough to fend of the hungry. People began to dip into the chowder pot with various containers: beer mugs, water glasses, coffee cups. A few of the more civilized managed to find a bowl. Sherm ate from a bright pink dog dish, borrowed from Vinny's basset hound.

The wine bottles began to empty, and in inverse proportion, the noise level began to rise. Marge was drunk again and dancing with Crazy Ed around the fire ring, a loose-kneed waltz that eventually landed them both face down in the sand.

The big biker turned a trash can upside down and, using the tire iron, did a credible job of drumming. Vinny joined in with his out-of-tune banjo.

"Play the harmonica for us, Jude," someone yelled.

Jude searched his pockets, found his Hohner, blew out the sand and salt water, and began to play.

The first note came out in a clear, mournful wail, a sound that only a harmonica or a human voice could produce. A song emerged, tugging at the memory with gentle familiarity and yet, its name refused to come to mind. But by whatever name it was known, a singing whale or a howling wolf would have recognized it and understood.

Vinny's fingers strumming the banjo strings came to a rest. Heavy ceased his drumming and leaned back, reminiscence clouding his eyes. While Jude's harmonica sang, no one spoke, stilled for a moment by the clean, honest sound of a man's soul speaking through his music.

Those who knew Jude and heard him play often wondered how this mild, unaffected man could express such haunting images with a simple melody and how he managed to steep each note in deep melancholy and sadness.

A half mile away, a crew working on an oil rig heard the sounds. When the noon whistle blew, the entire crew gathered on the edge of the highway. A big paunchy fellow in rank blue coveralls took off his filthy hard hat and combed back his hair with a four-fingered hand.

"Don't know about you fella's, but I'm goin' to that party."

"Me too," said his smaller companion. The rest followed, wide grins on their greasy faces.

The foreman watched them for a moment, then threw his spud-wrench into a nearby tool box. He jumped into his pickup. "Hey, guys, wait up. I'll give you a lift."

CHAPTER FOUR

T he sun completed the first half of its pilgrimage across the sky and began its descent toward nightfall. A breeze sprang up, drawing cool air in from the sea. With the shift in weather, Jude sensed a change in the timbre and dynamics of the party. Just as a flock of seabirds know that a tropical storm is about to become a hurricane, he knew this crowd was coalescing into critical mass. It swirled with fey energy, power that fed on sunlight and laughter, drawing onlookers into its vortex—sometimes against their better judgment.

Someone had set up a stereo, and the music washed away any vestige of silence. No shadows, no sadness, no shred of quiet that must be filled with self-contemplation. Adding to the din, a small truck with an engine that clanked like a bucket of rusty chains pulled in and parked near the entrance. A group of oil workers piled out, and their leader, a big fellow sporting a gargantuan paunch, spotted Jude. Leaving his comrades near the chowder pot, he crossed the courtyard, a smile stretched across his dirty face. He stopped in front of Jude, and his grin widened.

"I know you."

"Sorry, I don't remember," said Jude.

The man laughed. "About five years ago, Signal Hill. We were stripping down an old well. A cable snapped and whipped around the pump base we were working on. You got a knot on your head, and I lost this." He raised a hand, missing a forefinger. "You held the artery closed until the ambulance got there."

"You were skinnier then," said Jude.

"A damn sight so," said the man, laughing. "Thought we'd join the party. Don't care much for clam chowder, but I do like loud music and beer."

"There's plenty of both," said Jude.

The man gave Jude an appraising look. "You still got all your fingers and toes. You must have given up oil field work."

"Not completely," said Jude. "Just don't work regular."

"Only a crazy man works all the time." He shifted his feet. "Listen, if you need a job, this is a good crew. The foreman's an okay Joe and the rest—well they ain't geniuses, but they know how to watch out for their buddies."

"I'll keep it in mind," said Jude.

"Do that." The man pushed through the crowd and joined his friends near the alley behind the Shack.

Ellen returned from the pot with a beer mug full of chowder. "I simply cannot believe how tasty this stuff is."

"Fresh clams," said Jude. "That's the secret."

Across the courtyard, loud laughter caught Jude's attention. The oil workers had passed a greasy hard-hat among themselves and collected a few crumpled bills. A little fellow with missing teeth and a scar across his cheek emptied the money in Lonesome's lap. Laughing, she tucked the money in her pocket, tied her shirt up under her bosom exposing her lean midriff, and stepped out into an open space in the center. Her normally self-conscious expression disappeared, turning lively and full of confidence. Heavy, the big biker, began to beat a strong rhythm on his make-shift drums and Lonesome began to move — to belly dance.

Jude felt his jaw slacken. The Lonesome he knew walked like a drunken sailor and seemed to always be about to spill or drop something. Yet now she moved with grace and confidence. That a woman, constructed mainly of bone and stringy muscle, could suddenly become as sinuous as an eel stunned him.

The oil workers began to beat their hard hats against the concrete and whistle their encouragement. Lonesome responded with a smile.

Ellen put her hand on Jude's arm. "She dances quite well."

"Sure as hell does." He knew his response sounded inane even as he said the words. For all the years that Lonesome had lived on the beach, he'd never seen her dance — not a single step.

Ellen tightened her grip on his arm and snuggled closer.

"She's got great bones. If she fixed herself up, she could be a model."

The music changed to a tune unfamiliar to Jude, but it sounded classical, and it transformed Lonesome's demeanor. An oil worker reached to change the radio dial, but Sherm grabbed the man's hand and shook his head.

Lonesome's dark blue eyes turned misty, and she stopped dancing. A metamorphosis in her expression took place, breathtaking in its complexity. She went up on her toes, and her arms formed a graceful hoop over her head. Slowly, easily, a leg came up, and she whirled around in a movement Jude knew was both disciplined and practiced. He felt as if he'd just witnessed a great feat of sorcery, a stork transformed into a swan.

She performed a slow elegant pirouette, but it came to an abrupt end, and a grimace of pain wracked her face. Suddenly pale and drawn, she forced a smile and walked slowly back to the edge of the crowd. Sherman spun the radio dial, and a heavy Latin tempo filled the air.

Ellen grabbed Jude's arm and dragged him to his feet. "Come on. I'll teach you to Rumba."

He couldn't master the sexual intensity of the rhythm. Their legs tangled, and they both fell laughing. The older woman's make-up had disappeared, and her face was flushed with wine and excitement. The hard look in her eye had softened.

"I think I'd better sit down before I hurt myself," said Jude.

A man entered the courtyard from the street and stopped next to Jude. Salt deposits powdered his dark, leathery skin; his grizzled beard and hair were the color of frosted iron. Under one arm, he carried a battered surfboard. From his free hand hung a shirt with the tails pulled together to form a bag and the sleeves tied together to create a handle. The makeshift sack clinked as the clam shells inside collided. He leaned the surfboard against the wall of the Shack and scratched at a long, curving scar across his chest.

"Saw you guys digging clams this morning." He held up the shirt. "Thought I'd add these to the pot."

"They'll be welcome," said Jude. "There's beer by the barbecue, and a couple of jugs making the rounds."

"Think I'll have the beer," said the man. As he passed the chowder pot, he casually dumped in the clams.

Ellen looked resigned. "He didn't even wash them off."

"Doesn't matter," said Jude. "The sand will settle to the bottom."

"I'm sure it will," she said. "Where do you suppose he got that terrible scar?"

"Looks like a shark bite," said Jude.

Ellen shivered.

By late evening, the courtyard was jammed. The chowder pot was empty except for a sludge composed of wet sand and a few clam shells.

The makeup of the crowd had changed. Many of those present now were working class from one of the nearby inland cities; blue collars, hard hats, and business suits were about evenly mixed. They came here to relieve the boredom of their unchanging lives and to release some of the pressure generated by the constant striving to succeed. Sometimes their therapy tended to make life miserable for the local residents.

By sundown, a few fights had broken out, and Jude knew it would soon be time to go. He and the others who'd generated this storm would fade into the darkness taking with them its focus. They were the eye of the hurricane, and without them, the tempest would rapidly wane.

A man swaggered drunkenly to the fire ring and balanced himself precariously on its side. His white shirt billowed around his scrawny waist, and his cheap polyester tie hung askew. Thin as a starving ferret, his face flushed with drink, he glared at the crowd, his pale brown eyes exposing the yoked demons of resentment and rage. The man spread his legs, held his arms over his head, and howled — a challenge, brutish and primal. At that instant, Jude saw the butt of a revolver sticking out of the man's waistband.

Just what we need, he thought. A goddamn gunslinger. Every day Crazy Ed was improving, but if he saw that gun . . . Jude came to his feet, scanning the crowd. He had to find Ed before his friend saw the pistol.

When no one responded, Gunslinger stood with his hand hovering near the butt of his weapon, his eyes red and heated.

The moron probably wouldn't shoot anyone, except by accident, but just the sound of a pistol shot would be enough. Worried now, Jude pressed through the crowd. Where the hell was Ed?

Earlier, Jude had seen his friend enter the small alley behind the shack, probably headed for the toilet. He started toward it. From the corner of his eye, he saw Gunslinger draw the pistol and point it into the air. Turning, Jude drove forward, leaning at the waist.

The gun was bad enough, but if the idiot fired it . . . too late. A shot rang out, and someone screamed.

Using his shoulder as a ram, Jude slammed into the man just above the belt. A loud whoosh and Gunslinger fell backwards into the crowd. The pistol spun away from his grip.

Jude sprinted for the alley. Over his shoulder, he saw Heavy grab Gunslinger by the neck and lift him into the air, but Jude couldn't spare the idiot any more attention. He had to find his friend.

In the alley, his face waxen and still as death, stood Ed. Jude raced toward him, but Sherman arrived first, just as Ed's expression collapsed into frenzy and his body began to shudder violently. Sherm wrapped Ed in powerful arms, but in spite of his overpowering strength, was barely able to contain the man's kicking, writhing body. Jude dived and grabbed Ed's flailing feet.

"Get him into the Shack!" Jude shouted.

Lonesome opened the back door and held it while they dragged him through.

Inside, Vinny's new barmaid stood by the cash register, her eyes wide and frightened.

Somehow, they managed to wrestle Ed into a corner and pin him against the wall. He said nothing; the only sound he made was a guttural moan that came from behind his clenched teeth.

Jude took his hands. "Ed, look at me. Where are you?"

Ed's eyes rolled back, and violent spasms shook his body.

"Look at me," Jude repeated. "It's Jude and Sherm, your friends. You're in the Shack. No one is shooting at you. This isn't Vietnam."

Lonesome motioned to the barmaid. "Bring me some ice and wrap a towel around it."

The girl stood undecided, frightened. She seemed about to cry. Exasperated, Lonesome leaped over the bar, grabbed a handful of ice, wrapped it in a towel, and tossed it to Jude.

He wiped Ed's pallid face with the icy compress. The man gasped, and his breathing steadied.

"Open your eyes," Jude said softly. "Come on Ed. Pull out of it."

Crazy Ed didn't reply, but his thrashing body stilled, and Sherman loosened his grip a little.

Ed's body began to quiver as a great, gasping sob wracked his chest. Jude felt Ed return the grip on his hands. "Where are you, Ed?"

"The—the Shack." Ed's teeth chattered on the words.

Lonesome knelt down beside Jude and leaned past him to brush Ed's lank hair from his face.

"Everyone here's a friend," she said. "You come back to us, you hear?"

All Ed could manage was a nod. His breathing fell into a steady rhythm, and his eyes regained their focus.

Wino Willy came through the back door carrying a small bottle. He squatted by Ed and held it out. "It's peach brandy, the kind you like best."

Ed reached out a hand, but it shook so badly he couldn't hold the flask. Willy unscrewed the cap and held it to his friend's lips. Ed took a big gulp and coughed. He managed a feeble grin.

"Where did you get peach brandy?"

"Found it," said Willy.

Ed's grin grew stronger. "Hope somebody lost it first."

"Don't matter," said Jude. "How you doing now?"

"Okay." He struggled out of Sherman's arms and wiped his face with shaking hands. "Think I'll go lay down for a while. This damn party's out of control anyway." He leaned heavily on Sherman's shoulder as he stood up.

"I'll walk with you," said Lonesome.

"Me too." Sherman stood up. "Too many inlanders to have fun." He wiped his mouth. "Besides, you got good stuff to drink."

Willy pulled Jude aside. "I'm going to disappear for awhile. If the cops show up and ask questions about someone shoplifting brandy . . ."

"You've been with me all day."

"Thanks." Willy scooted out the back door and into the dark.

Heavy appeared in the front door with a big hand wrapped tightly around Gunslinger's neck. He held the man as casually as one might hold an errant puppy.

"What you wanna do with this guy?"

"Just hang on to him till the cops get here," said Jude.

"Don't really want to talk to the cops." Heavy scowled at Gunslinger. "How bout I tie him to the back of my bike and drag him up and down the street a couple a times?"

Jude laughed. "Not a bad idea, but he ain't worth the trouble."

Vinny came through the front door holding Gunslinger's pistol. He gestured with his crutch.

"Just toss him in the corner. I'll keep an eye on him till the cops pick him up."

The word toss was probably ill-advised, as Heavy followed his instructions to the letter. The building shook when Gunslinger struck the far wall. He groaned and cradled his head, but made no attempt to flee.

Heavy dusted his hands as he walked back to the door. "Good party. How's the crazy man doing?"

"Gone home," said Jude.

Heavy nodded. "Good." He started out, paused, and turned. "You tell him next time I come by, maybe me an him talk business."

"I'll pass it on," said Jude.

With a huge sigh of contentment, Heavy disappeared into the dark.

Jude looked around and saw Ellen standing in the back door, her face pale. She looked disheveled and tired. Taking her arm, he led her outside to a quiet place overlooking the ocean.

"You want to take a walk on the beach?"

She stopped and looked up at him. Her lips quivered when she spoke.

"I don't think so." Turning away she wiped her eyes. "Will your friend be all right?"

"He'll survive."

"That moron with the gun frightened me," she said. "But your friend seemed to go . . ."

"Crazy," Jude finished. "That's why we call him Crazy Ed."

She turned, faced him, and placed her hand lightly on his chest.

"I'll be honest with you, Jude. I came down here today to find some young stud to hop into the sack with." Her eyes held his. "You already know that of course, but I had to say it."

"You've changed your mind I take it?"

"Yes, but—"

"If you say I'm too nice a guy, I'll puke."

She giggled. "I'm sorry. I almost did." Her expression sobered. "But the truth is—it's your eyes. I feel as if you're looking right through me." She shook her head as if what she'd said proved inadequate. "You hold people up to the light, Jude, and I can't survive that kind of scrutiny."

When he didn't respond, she let her hand drop from his chest. "You've heard that before too, haven't you?"

The silence stretched out and she sighed. "It's not just you, Jude. I took a huge gulp of life today and almost choked on it."

Jude leaned over and kissed her gently on the cheek. "Better get going. It's a long way back to the real world."

As she walked away, she turned, gave him a wry smile, and waved.

"Watch out for the giant killer clam."

When she disappeared into the darkness, he turned toward the beach. A delicate breeze blew in his face bringing the salty, iodine odor of the sea.

Waves rolled in, edged with pale-green phosphorescence, and on their retreat, left a lacework of wan luminescence on the sand. In the feeble light, he saw a woman walking near the edge of the surf. Abruptly, she stopped and faced out to sea. Her chin lifted, and for an instant, defiance and anger marked every nuance of her carriage. Although she looked familiar, it took a few minutes for the memory to connect. It came to him with a jolt, Shelly, Cowboy Toby's mother.

While he watched, she took a sheet of paper from her pocket, crumpled it, and threw it into the sea. Her defiance evaporated, and she knelt down in the shallow water, put her hands to her face, and began to weep.

CHAPTER FIVE

Jude stood, stunned and uncertain while Shelly knelt in the edge of the surf, her body shaking with sobs. The poem in his shirt pocket seemed to be burning its way into his heart.

Oh God, if there be a God, take me instead.

For an instant, he was looking down at himself, in another place, and long ago. Yet time was a sorcerer making it seem only yesterday. As powerful as the day it was spawned, he remembered his own shattering grief, a nineteen-year-old boy on his knees next to a new casket, poised over a raw wound in the earth.

Those memories kept him from rushing to her, kept his feet rooted in the sand. If he went to her side, if he spoke to her, she would verify a truth already being whispered in his ear by a fiend called reason. And when he knew, part of her heartache would become his.

As if being crushed from above, Shelly bent slowly forward until her head almost touched her knees. He heard a sound, a deep, primal moan wrenched slowly from her soul. She needed someone to comfort her—anyone. But again, the powerful specters of his own sorrow enervated him, the bridge between mind and body swept away by a flood of memories. Desperately, he tried to close off the deluge, but the gate was open, and pain rushed out.

He took a deep breath and felt the note press against his chest. With a terrible effort, he raised one foot and put it in front of the other. Then repeated with the other. Deep inside, a voice whispered that sharing her anguish would bring about his own season of torment, but still he continued.

Eventually, he was beside her. He knelt down. "It's me, Shelly. Jude." Gently, he rested his arm across her thin, quivering shoulders.

She raised her head. Even in the darkness, he could see the smudges of exhaustion under her eyes. And nothing could possibly hide the grief.

"Toby?"

He had to force the name between his lips.

She nodded. "My little boy."

The words seemed so simple, and yet Jude suddenly ached as if all the sorrow in the world lay on his heart. "Do you want to tell me, or would you rather I leave you alone?"

"Stay." It was more a gasp of pain than a word. "But I have no right to unload on you, Jude."

He gathered her in his arms. "I just gave you the right."

For a while, she cried against his chest, then words began to form between the sobs.

"All those chemicals were supposed to save him. But they aren't working."

"Where is he now?"

Leaning back from him, she wiped her eyes. "He's in the hospital. They're going to try one last time." Her eyes held his. "I had to give them more money."

"The bastards."

She shook her head. "No, they're not bastards, Jude. Just people trying to do their job. They were sympathetic, but they needed at least a token payment. I owe them so much."

Turning her head away, she stared out across the dark ocean. He could smell her tear-wet hair.

"When will he get out?"

"Tomorrow." Her voice was barely audible. "By noon, I think. In time for his birthday."

The words struck Jude like a gust of cold wind. "His bicycle?"

"I don't even have enough money left to buy him a birthday cake."

Sickness spread through Jude, and he swallowed hard. "How much is the bike?"

A tremulous smile fluttered and disappeared. "It's nearly a hundred dollars, Jude." She let her head rest on his chest as if she could draw strength from his heartbeat. "Ninety-seven dollars and ninety-nine cents."

Hopelessness almost overwhelmed him. That was more money than he'd possessed at any one time in a year. "I'll see what I can do."

This time, her smile was less fleeting. "You're a generous man, Jude. But you know, it's hopeless." She arose and scrubbed her face with the sleeve of her blouse. "I've got to get ready to go to work."

Jude stood up with her and brushed a glob of sand from her cheek.

Again, she smiled, and her plain grief-ravaged face became strong and beautiful.

"Don't worry about it, Jude. You and your friends have problems of your own." She patted his arm and started back up the beach.

Her departure left Jude feeling hollow and useless. A wave rolled in, and cool water curled playfully around his ankles. There had to be a way of raising cash. Given time, he could find a job and earn the money, but time had, without warning, become a grim, uncompromising enemy.

For a while, he walked along the beach. Ideas for acquiring the bicycle buzzed and circled in his mind like angry hornets. But he discarded them all; some for their impracticability, others for their sheer silliness, and a few because of serious legal complications.

After a time, he found himself near the northern limit of Sunset Beach. Just beyond lay the gated community of Surfside where those with money, talent, or power chose to live. In the dark, it resembled a pile of children's blocks, petulantly discarded and forgotten. He knew from experience there would be no help from society's thin upper layer. They were too wealthy and too self-involved to concern themselves with the plight of one little boy. If this was to be done, it would have to be by him and those like him, who had little to give.

His own apartment was nearby, and he turned reluctantly toward it. Apartment, he thought wryly. A converted one car garage just barely filling the legal requirements of a rental. It fronted an alley, wedged between two like structures; one still used as a garage, the other a storage bin.

The door stood ajar, but that didn't concern him. He never locked it; he had nothing worth stealing. A lock and key would have been meaningless complications.

Pushing the door open, he switched on the light, half expecting to find one of his friends asleep on the floor. No one. The room, lit by a single bulb hanging from the ceiling, was depressingly empty. His small cot, covered by a worn sleeping bag, appeared just as he'd left it the day before. In one corner, a cheap plastic shower curtain closed off a rudimentary toilet and shower. On the wall, a mismatched pair of swim fins—one green the other blue—hung from a nail. The concrete floor was unadorned except for a threadbare beach towel spread near the entrance of the shower.

He sat on the cot and stared at the floor, as if it would provide inspiration. There was nothing to see except what might be the tracks of a cockroach crossing a patch of dust. Must be a pretty dumb cockroach, he mused. There hasn't been a trace of food in this room for weeks.

A search of his pockets turned up his harmonica, an old single bladed pocket knife, and a comb with three missing teeth. Not a single penny. He'd spent all the money he borrowed from Willy, although that was not too surprising. He usually did. But this time, his own lack of accountability saddened him.

Nothing he owned was worth a hundred dollars even if it were new, and nothing was. Reaching under his bed, he pulled out a cardboard box. The sum of the last ten years of his life lay in that carton. He sighed. It seemed smaller than he remembered. Every year, the tally of his belongings shrank, and more of the artifacts from his past slipped into oblivion. Would there come a time when he owned nothing? Would he himself dwindle into nothingness?

On top lay a pair of faded blue jeans, his dress attire. Below that was an eclectic collection of T-shirts, socks, and underclothes. He reached beneath all the clothes and pulled out a thick hardcover book. Bound in dark red buckram, it had The Adventures of Huckleberry Finn scribed in gold leaf across both the cover and the spine.

The book was his prized possession. His grandmother had given it to him on his twelfth birthday, and he'd read it at least twenty times.

But even if he could bring himself to sell it, the book wasn't a collector's item. Slowly, his finger traced the worn title.

"Jeez, Huck. You at least had a life."

Carefully, he restored the book to its place and pushed the box back beneath his bed. How could he possibly raise a hundred dollars before Toby came home from the hospital tomorrow? Vinny would supply the money if he had it, but Jude knew he didn't. Like the rest of the beach crowd, Vinny lived day to day, just barely surviving. He gave away too much beer and rented his rooms too cheaply to make any semblance of profit. No, Vinny wasn't the answer.

A hesitant tap on the door interrupted his musing. He yanked the door open, and a startled Lonesome took a step back. "I'm sorry, Jude. If there's someone with you, I'll leave." She flushed deeply and started to go.

"No, come on in." Jude was puzzled by her uncharacteristic diffidence.

As she stepped through the door, she looked around his small room and seemed relieved by what she saw.

"What's the matter, Lonesome?"

She took a small bottle of Red River from beneath her shirt. "Crazy Ed crashed in my bed. I thought maybe it would be okay if I slept on your floor." She opened the bottle and passed it to him.

He took it and sipped. "You can have my bed. Don't think I'll be sleeping much tonight."

A look of concern crossed her face. "What's wrong?"

"It's Toby."

"Oh, God." She sat down on the bed. "Is he . . .?"

"In the hospital." Jude sat down beside her. "He's there for another one of his treatments, but now, Shelly doesn't have the money to buy a bike for his birthday."

He took the folded paper from his pocket and gave it to Lonesome.

She read it and looked up at him. "Shelly wrote this?"

"Yes."

Lonesome quickly turned her face away, but not before he saw the tears spring to her eyes. The sight shocked him nearly as much as seeing her belly dance. He'd been with her the night she'd been hit by a drunk driver and broke her arm. Not one tear had escaped her then, not even when the emergency room doctor set the bone before the anesthetics took effect.

She was struggling for control so that he wouldn't see her distress, so he pretended not to notice. Making a big show of sipping the wine, he coughed, scrubbed his eyes, and passed her the bottle.

She followed his example and surreptitiously wiped her own eyes.

"What are we going to do?"

"Somehow, we're going to raise a hundred bucks and buy that bicycle."

She snorted. "A hundred? How the hell we going to do that? Rob a bank?"

"That's on my list," he said.

She gave him a dark look. "This is one time, I might consider it a viable option." With a sigh, she leaned back against the rolled towel he used as a pillow. "Ouch." Reaching under her thigh, she picked up the knife, harmonica, and comb and gave him a quizzical look.

"Everything I own," he said. "I've simplified my life."

"Maybe oversimplified." She gave him a wry smile. "I should talk. Everything I own would fit in a purse—if I had one."

Her eyes lost their focus, and her voice softened. "You ever wonder what it's like to live a normal life."

Jude took the harmonica and slipped it back into his pocket. "I don't even remember what normal is."

"That's what scares me," she said. "Neither do I."

Jude put his hand around the back of her neck and shook her lightly. "I know how you feel. Let's find Willy. Maybe he's got some money left."

"Forget it," said Lonesome. "He didn't even have enough to buy that bottle of brandy he gave Ed."

"Let's find him anyway, and Sherm and Ed too. Maybe we can figure something out."

"Christ, Jude. We're dropouts. None of us could find our butts if the rest were holding flashlights and shouting instructions."

"That's true," he said. "But we are all we've got."

Outside, a warm, damp breeze drifted in from the sea, enclosing the street lights in vaporous coronas. As they passed Old Dan's restaurant, Lonesome slowed and gave Jude a musing look.

"Let's ask Old Dan if he would contribute a little money. He's a nice man."

"He is a business man," said Jude. "If you buy from him, he's nice."

"You're a cynic." She turned toward the restaurant door.

Jude knew the argument was hopeless. Although she could be formidably pragmatic, Lonesome invariably refused to be a pessimist.

Inside, only two booths were occupied, and a man wearing a trucker's cap sat at the small counter. Dessy, the waitress, came out of the kitchen with a coffee pot in hand, saw them, sighed loudly with exasperation, and walked to the nearest table without speaking. Jude knew the woman possessed a bloated sense of self-importance and despised him for refusing to acknowledge her superiority.

She poured coffee for the seated couple; every movement of her chunky body radiating supremacy. Jude often wondered what chemical she used on her hair to produce the color and texture of dead grass.

She turned abruptly, slopping coffee and affecting the stance of a rankled but patient matriarch.

"Want a booth, or are you going to eat at the counter?"

"We're looking for Dan," said Lonesome.

"He ain't here. Went to check on the San Diego restaurant. Won't be back for a couple of days."

"Maybe you could help," said Lonesome. "We're trying to raise money to buy little Toby a bike for his birthday - "

"Forget it," Dessy snapped. "This isn't a charity, and I'm busy."

In the entire restaurant, Jude counted only five people.

"Fact is," said Dessy, "I don't know why Dan even lets you people come in here. I wouldn't."

"The money's not for us," said Jude. "It's for a sick little boy."

"He ain't mine. I didn't get knocked up and have to raise a kid alone."

"Toby's father was killed in Vietnam," said Lonesome.

Dessy rolled her eyes in exaggerated resignation. "Doesn't really matter does it?" She gave them a patronizing smile. "Shelly hasn't got a husband, and that's her problem. Let her buy the kid his toys. She thinks she's such a great waitress. Makes more in tips in one night than I make in a week."

Through the swinging doors from the kitchen, the bus boy slipped into the room. He gave Jude a timid grin and reached into his pocket.

"Pedro, get back in the kitchen," Dessy snapped. "You got dishes to wash."

Pedro's expression went flat and emotionless, and he pushed back through the swinging doors. Over his shoulder, he shot Dessy a look that was a strange combination of pity and anger.

Dessy waved the pot at the front door, slopping more coffee. "If you're not going to eat, leave. I don't have time for this."

Jude took Lonesome's arm and led her outside. Her face was pale with suppressed fury.

"How can that woman stand herself?"

"She can't," he said.

Downcast, Lonesome stared at a flattened soft drink can at her feet. Suddenly, savagely, she kicked it. She looked up, her expression hurt and vulnerable. "We're not going to get any help from anyone, are we?"

"I never really thought it would be any other way."

They found Wino Willy at his favorite retreat — an old driftwood stump that provided a view of Anaheim Bay. It wasn't a place of great beauty.

At night, the dark water looked like oil, and the odor of decaying vegetation made the air almost unbreathable. No one came here at night, except Willy, and Jude suspected that was why the man loved it. They told Willy their plan to help Toby.

"Yeah, I'll help," said Willy. "If life shits on us, it's usually our own fault, but that little boy deserves better."

The three made their way across the highway to a shed behind the boat service dock. Sherm and Lonesome had been living there for a couple of years, but as they approached, Jude realized he'd never been inside. Not that it mattered; it was, after all, just a place to sleep.

Inside they found Sherm practicing his letters on a writing pad, and Jude looked over his shoulder. The letters were scrawled but recognizable. He put his hand on the big man's arm.

"How's it coming, Sherm?"

Sherman didn't look up. "Okay. I'm up to 'W'. Lonesome say I only got three to go."

Jude noticed there were two beds, separated by a ragged curtain. Ed lay on one of them, muddled and groggy but awake. When he saw Lonesome, he roused himself and sat on the floor.

"Sorry I took your bed. Just conked out."

"Forget it," she said. "None of us are going to sleep tonight anyway."

Sherm looked up expectantly. "Nuther party?"

"Nope," replied Jude. He explained about Toby and the bicycle.

"Damnit," said Ed. "How the hell we going to get that kind of money?"

No one answered his question for there seemed to be no answer.

The quiet drew out until Sherman stirred and cleared his throat. "Old Hal got a sign out front of his bait shop."

"What does it say?" asked Jude patiently.

"Too many words," said Sherman. "But it the same sign he use long time ago when he buy mackerel."

Ed jumped up and banged his head on the low ceiling. He sat down again, rubbing his growing bump.

"That's it, Jude. Remember, a couple a years ago. The old son-of-a-bitch ran out of mackerel for bait."

"He bought from anybody who had them to sell." Willy did a little jig. "At fifty cents a pound."

Lonesome excitedly whacked Jude on the shoulder. "And he wasn't checking for a license."

"It's a start." Jude paced the small room. "Now we have to figure out how to get our hands on some mackerel."

CHAPTER SIX

B ecause the shed was an abandoned ice house from a time before refrigeration, it was spartan but well insulated and comfortable in almost any weather. The owner of the repair dock allowed Sherm and Lonesome to sleep there in return for Sherm's presence as a deterrent to potential thieves. Although narrow with a low ceiling, rather than feeling cramped, the small space provided the friends with a sense of unity.

Jude moved to the rear where a single-pane window looked out over the marina. A light breezed crinkled the water, and boats tied up at the dock swayed gently.

"There's usually mackerel at the Seal Beach pier," said Willy. "But it's a long walk, and there's no guarantee we would catch anything."

"Besides," Ed added, "we would need rods and reels to fish a pier."

Jude turned around. "We need a boat." The others sat watching him expectantly. "We ruled out a pier, and mackerel aren't going to flop up on land and wait for us to pick them up."

"Got no boat," said Sherm.

Again, it grew quiet, and Jude began to despair. His own brain seemed to be thick and useless, like a bowl of oatmeal. A headache throbbed behind his eyes with increasing intensity.

Willy cleared his throat. "There's that old, abandoned dory under the bridge."

"Jeez, Willy," said Ed. "That thing's rotten."

"Yeah, it's in pretty bad shape," Willy agreed.

"Wait." Jude began pacing again. "We've got to give every idea a fair shake. Let's walk down and take a look at it."

"Got nothing to lose," said Lonesome.

The half mile walk would have been, in ordinary circumstances, a pleasant diversion. But the small group progressed quietly; preoccupied and drawn into themselves. Jude wondered if Toby's plight had instilled in the others his own sense of diminishment. This small, gentle boy's courage and serenity had brought a new perspective to Jude's own existence.

Frustration bit at Jude's gut. A little blue bicycle did not seem to be a great deal to ask of life.

Pacific Coast Highway crossed Anaheim Bay on a long, curving concrete span that, to the locals, became the demarcation between the outer and back bay. Under the southern terminus, transients frequently spent the night; the odor of their trash and urine made the place almost unbearable.

Jude remembered the dory as being half submerged, but someone had pulled it up on shore, and it sat on its side, well above the high-water line. At first glance, its condition appeared hopeless; a basketball-sized hole gaped in the bottom. However, the time spent on land had dried the wood and slowed decay.

Grabbing the gunwale, Jude shook it. Nothing came loose.

"Let's drag it out under that streetlight so we can see."

Light did nothing to enhance the dory's appearance. About fifteen feet from bow to stern, it had been constructed of plywood on a hardwood frame. The paint was gone, the plywood was beginning to delaminate, and the keel board was warped and loose. A layer of dried mud filled the starboard side.

Jude picked up a discarded can.

"The frame members I can see don't look too bad. Need to get rid of some of this gunk so we can see the rest." He began to scrape away the debris.

Lonesome grabbed a small board and helped. Sherm found the remnants of a cast-off bathing suit and used it to finish the cleaning job.

Rubbing his back, Jude stood up and surveyed the boat.

"The frame is sound. Some of the plywood's pretty rotten."

"Don't look good to me," said Willy.

One by one, they seated themselves in a circle around the boat and stared at it. Lonesome tossed a rock through the gash in the bottom. "We need a piece of plywood big enough to patch that hole."

"And some screws to hold it," added Ed.

"Probably going to need caulking compound in the seams," said Willy.

Sherm pursed his lips and thought for a moment. "Need big bucket."

"Bucket?" Willy looked confused.

"To bail out with," said Sherm.

Tossing aside a stick he'd used to clean out the smaller areas, Ed gave the boat a disgusted look.

"It's impossible. If we had a lot of time and some money, we might get this thing to float."

Lonesome gave Jude a hopeful look. "You think we can fix it?"

"No, Ed's right. We can't fix it—but we can get it to float."

That brought a disbelieving look from Willy. "You got a magic wand we don't know about?"

"What we need," said Jude, "is a big waterproof tarp."

Ed stared at the dory for a second, then looked at Jude.

"I think I know what you're getting at. It might work."

"It would have to be heavy," said Lonesome.

Sherm nodded. "Real heavy."

Willy looked from one face to the other.

"Would somebody explain this wonderful idea to me?"

Jude swept his hands apart.

"We cover the outside of the whole damn thing with one piece of waterproof canvas. No seams, no leaks."

Open mouthed, Willy stared at the boat. "I'll be damned."

"We still need to find a tarp," said Lonesome.

Ed stood up suddenly and jammed his hands in his pockets. He stalked down to the water's edge and stared out into the darkness with an intensity that worried Jude.

He came back and sat down. "I know where there's a tarp just like one we need."

"I don't think I'm going to like this," said Jude.

A genuine grin on Ed's face was a rarity, but this one was full of sincere humor.

"The rich guy's construction site in Surfside. They dumped a big load of lumber yesterday and covered it with a tarp."

"Oh, Christ," said Willy. "The rich guy's got an armed guard there at night."

"Sure as hell." Ed looked stubborn. "But I'm going in there and gettin' that tarp."

Lonesome grabbed Ed's arm. "You can't. They've got fences and alarms and lights all around."

Jude drew Ed aside. "I don't think this is a good idea."

"Probably not," Ed agreed. "Good ideas aren't my strong suit." The jovial demeanor evaporated. "But I'm going to do it."

"Then I'm going in with you."

The grin was back. "You're too damned stubborn. I need someone who'll go along with my plan."

Although Ed was inches taller than Jude, for an instant, they were eye to eye. Jude could see the determination in Ed's every gesture, yet there was more here than simple tenacity.

"Okay," Jude said. "After all, it was the rich guy's own idea. He said if you want something, you got to reach out and take it. I'll help however I can."

"Thanks." Ed turned to Sherm. "Sherm, you and I have got the hard part. You game, pardner?"

"Okay," said Sherm.

"If Jude goes, I go," said Lonesome.

Willy got up and gave Ed a resigned look. "Guess we might as well all go to jail together."

"Jail's not all that bad," said Ed. "Come on. We haven't got all night."

The construction site was at the South end of Surfside, a ten-minute walk from their present position. They moved quietly, following Ed without conversation. Ed's skill as he moved stealthily among the shadows, astonished Jude.

Where the highway curved away from Surfside, they were forced to detour around bright yellow barricades that surrounded a deep trench. Ducking under the barricade, Willy peered down into the ditch.

"This damn thing's over ten feet deep."

"New sewer line for the rich guy's house," said Lonesome. "There were warning lights here yesterday. Somebody must have stolen them."

"Come on," said Jude. "We need to get that boat in the water by midnight or we won't get any mackerel."

Surfside consisted of an eclectic assortment of houses and apartments clustered so tightly that the streets became claustrophobic alleys and the alleys dark, narrow pathways. At night, thick shadows lay everywhere, relieved by occasional rectangles of butter-yellow light from open windows. The strains of classical piano, played expertly and with flair, flowed in from somewhere around.

The construction site was a large lot overlooking the ocean. A ten-foot chain-link fence topped with razor wire surrounded it, broken only by a wide, sliding gate fronting the street. At each corner, a stanchion supported a bright light. The only construction to date was a concrete slab with plumbing stubs rising up like dead weeds. Behind the slab sat a portable toilet, and next to it, a pile of lumber covered with a heavy tarp. Near the fence, a metal tool shed cast its shadow over the lumber. Just inside the gate stood a small, glass-fronted guard kiosk, which at the moment was empty.

The group gathered in a tiny alley with a view of the front gate.

"There's no guard," Willy said hopefully.

"He's here somewhere," said Jude. "There's a lunch pail in the shack."

Just then, the door to the portable toilet opened, and the guard walked out into the light. He paused and straightened his gun belt of thick black leather, buffed to a high gloss. A big, nickel plated revolver hung from one side; from the other, a baton, a can of mace, and handcuffs. His uniform of blue and gray had been pressed and creased until it reflected light. His black, high-topped boots shone like wet glass; brass buttons and epaulet decorations gleamed with recent polish.

"Holy shit," said Jude.

For a while, no one else seemed to be able to express themselves.

"Jeez," Willy whispered. "The son-of-a-bitch even shines his bullets."

The guard turned toward the light. His heavy face dwarfed bulbous, vacuous eyes, set deep under the brow ridges of a lowland gorilla. A tiny, thin-lipped mouth stretched itself in a chilling, mirthless smile. He walked toward the guard kiosk, his hand hovering near the butt of his revolver. Jude glanced at Ed. The tall man's face was pallid and dank with sweat.

"I think we better let this one go," Jude said.

Slowly but decisively, Ed shook his head.

"No." Using his sleeve, he wiped his brow. "Sherm, I weigh about a hundred seventy. Can you lift me up to the top of that fence?"

Sherm squinted and looked thoughtful. "Yup. Maybe can't hold you long."

"One second will be enough." He scanned the site one more time. "Willy, you go to the left side. Gather up some wood, paper, anything that will burn. When you get a signal from Jude, set it on fire."

"Got no matches," said Willy.

Ed took a cheap butane lighter out of his pocket. "Use this." He put his hand on Jude's shoulder. "You stay here buddy, you and Lonesome. When I give you the thumbs-up signal, you pass it on to Willy. He won't be able to see me."

"You're not giving us much to do," said Jude.

"You guys will be my backup. If things get really screwed up, I can count on you to come up with something."

"How about an explanation at least," said Lonesome.

"Sherm's going to lift me high enough to go over the fence between those lights on the right. I'll grab the tarp and toss it over the fence to Sherm. When you see my signal, pass it on to Willy, and he'll light the fire. While the guard's distracted by the fire, I'll go out the front gate."

Jude took Ed's arm.

"He has a gun, Ed."

"I intend to keep that in mind. If everything goes right, that idiot will never know we've been here." He stepped back from the entrance to the alley. "Come on, Sherm."

When the two men were out of sight, Lonesome spoke softly.

"If that moron pulls his gun, Ed's liable to flip out."

"I know. But for some reason, he needs to do this."

"What if things go wrong?"

"You up to jumping a man with a gun?"

"Hell no. But that's what you intend to do, and I'll be right with you."

"Let's hope we don't have to."

The guard stood in his tiny shack at parade rest, staring dully out into the darkness. His infuriating half smile never left his face.

A few minutes passed, and Ed appeared in the side street with a sheet of cardboard tucked into his belt. Sherm followed a few steps behind. Ed moved toward the fence with a gait so slow and smooth, that he almost seemed not to be in motion.

Sherm followed, imitating Ed's actions like a bear mimicking a gazelle. The guard stirred, stared down at his lunch pail a moment, checked his watch, and resumed his vigilant stance.

Ed reached the fence and motioned to Sherm. The big man kneeled and braced his hands on his hips. Ed carefully stepped up onto his shoulders and balanced himself. Sherm seemed to be staring off into the distance but slowly, deliberately he stood up. When fully erect, he brought his hands up to his shoulders, and carefully, Ed placed his feet in the big man's palms.

Muscles in Sherm's arms bunched and knotted. Slowly, Ed began to rise. Tremors ran through Sherm's arms and Ed lurched, once, twice. He regained his balance and stood unmoving. Again, Sherm's powerful arms began to straighten. Ed's waist came even with the top of the fence. He unfolded the piece of cardboard, placed it over the razor wire, and without hesitation, rolled over it. While airborne, he did a complete flip and landed on his feet in the shadows of the tool shed.

The sound he made caused the guard to look around. But Ed didn't move, blending into the shadows. After a few seconds, the guard turned back to stare out of the gate.

"Ed's done that before," Jude whispered.

Moving faster now, Ed slipped through the shadows toward the lumber. Quickly but carefully, he rolled the tarp back, folded it into a compact bundle, and carried it to the fence. He started to throw, changed his mind, and repositioned his feet.

The guard turned and picked up his lunch pail.

Ed froze.

With movements as deliberate and sluggish as a tree sloth, the guard opened his lunch pail and began to remove its contents. Jude knew Ed wouldn't be able to hold that position much longer.

Scraping the ground with his foot, he uncovered several small pebbles. He picked up a handful, selected one and threw. It missed. Another stone and another miss. Lonesome pushed him gently aside. She took a pebble from his hand, concentrated, wound up, and threw. It bounced off the glass with a loud ping. The guard paused with a sandwich almost in his mouth.

Jude counted three before the man responded. Carefully placing the sandwich back in the lunch pail, the guard moved to the window with his back to Ed.

Ed tossed the tarp. It flew upward and almost cleared the fence. One corner caught on the razor wire just long enough to flip the clumsy bundle in mid-flight. As it descended, Sherm jumped, caught the unwieldy mess, and staggered back. Part of the tarp flapped over his head. Blindly, he stumbled into the alley, and just as he disappeared into the darkness, Jude saw him trip.

The sound was like a buffalo stampede in a tin can factory. Although he couldn't see, Jude surmised Sherm had fallen over a garbage pail.

Inside the kiosk, the guard paused again, this time holding a potato chip just outside his open mouth. Again, Jude counted three before the man responded. Deliberately, the man closed his mouth, replaced the chip, and stood up. As he stepped out of the guard shack, he unbuckled the strap over his pistol. For exactly three seconds, he stared at the alley, then his head turned, surveillance-camera fashion, and he spent three more on the tool shed.

"I didn't see where Ed went," said Jude.

"The tool shanty," said Lonesome.

"Shit." Someone had spilled a bag of dry concrete in front of the shed, and a small cloud of telltale dust hung in the air.

Eventually, the fact that the dust didn't rise by itself penetrated the guard's consciousness. Drawing his pistol, he moved forward slowly in an exaggerated squat, holding the big revolver with both hands. The emotionless half-smile twitched and writhed.

"We've got to do something," said Lonesome.

"Try another rock," said Jude.

She took a larger stone and threw. It struck the glass with a satisfying ring. "Damnit," she said. "I hoped it would break."

The guard either didn't hear or ignored the sound. He continued forward, his eyes glittering with expectation.

Jude turned toward Willy. The young man held his hands in a pleading gesture. He pointed to a mass of paper piled against the fence. Jude gave him the thumbs-up sign.

While Willy tried to light the fire, Jude began to look for a club. All he found was a chunk of broken concrete. Lonesome did better with a discarded mop handle.

Willy had a fire going, but the flames were small, and there was no smoke. The guard was within feet of the tool shed door.

Jude looked at Lonesome. "You ready?"

She nodded.

Suddenly, the guard rushed forward, grabbed the door, and yanked it open. He jumped back and leveled his pistol. From out of the dark shed came a tall shadow. It fell forward and struck the pile of dry concrete, raising a cloud of chalky dust.

The guard followed the falling object with his pistol. He now stood poised, his sick smile wide and expectant. When the dust cleared, a big scoop shovel lay in front of him, prostrate, groveling for its life.

Apparently, the guard suffered from a sensory overload that increased his information processing time. It took four seconds for him to lower the pistol and two more to straighten up with a vaguely disappointed look on his face. The half-smile returned to being merely infuriating.

Willy had fanned his small fire into a respectable blaze and finally, it penetrated the guards overloaded brain. He turned and peered for the allotted three counts, then trotted toward the fire.

Inside the tool shed, a dark figure dropped from over the door, and Ed peered out.

The guard reached the fence and stood staring.

"Ed's got three seconds," said Jude.

He only used up two. Without breaking his stride, he streaked through the gate and flopped down beside Lonesome, gasping for breath. His pale face shone with fine beads of sweat, and his hands trembled.

Lonesome smacked his arm hard enough to make him wince. "You scared the shit outta me." Instantly contrite, she put her arm around shoulder and held him. "I'm sorry, Ed."

Ed looked down at his hands; his fingers trembled so badly, they almost seemed to have a life of their own. He took a deep breath and held them in front of his face. Slowly but inexorably, the shaking ceased.

He gave her a triumphant smile. "I did it."

"You sure as hell did," said Jude. "Just like a professional."

A strange sound caught their attention. Willy's fire blazed to the top of the fence, and a light breeze strewed sparks and burning paper. In a futile attempt to put it out, the guard was kicking at the fence, scattering the fire more effectively than the breeze.

Running footsteps came from the back of the alley and Willy appeared. He dropped down by Ed and slapped him on the back. "Nice going."

Jude reached out to Ed. "Need a hand?"

Ed held his eyes for just an instant. "Yes, I did. Thanks."

"Let's get the hell out of here," said Willy. He looked around. "Where's Sherm?"

Ed climbed to his feet. "I told him we'd meet him at the boat."

CHAPTER SEVEN

In deference to Ed's successful campaign, the small group made no attempt to hide their movements as they threaded their way through the dark streets. They walked proudly and openly as befitted conquering heroes.

As they neared the highway, a sound caused Jude to call a halt. It came again, a cross between the mating call of an elk and a sonic boom. "What the hell was that?"

"It's Sherm," Lonesome said. "That's the way he sounds when he sneezes."

Jude glanced around, but all he could see was the barricades around the open sewer trench.

"Oh shit." He broke into a run.

At the edge of the trench, he stopped and looked down. Just visible at the bottom, Sherm sat on the folded tarp.

He looked up, wiping his nose on his sleeve. "Took you long time."

The rest of the group gathered behind Jude.

"You okay?" asked Ed.

"Yup. Sawdust make me sneeze."

"Can you climb out?" asked Lonesome.

"Nope," said Sherm, shaking his head. "Can't get out."

Willy lay on his stomach and reached down, but Sherm had fallen in the deepest part, and even standing, his grip fell a foot short of meeting Willy's.

Lonesome dropped down, but her longer arms also failed to reach Sherm's open hand. She got up and dusted her shirt. "We need a rope or something."

At that moment, a car door slammed. Behind them on the highway shoulder sat an old flatbed pickup with battered plywood sideboards enclosing the bed. An assortment of gardening tools hung or stood inside.

A stout, brown-faced man climbed out of the passenger side. Another man exited the driver's side and began unfastening something from the pickup bed.

"Good evening, Señor," said the closest man. He climbed over the barriers and flashed a warm smile. "Me and my cousin, Julio, we come over the bridge and see a man fall in that hole." He held out his hand. "I am Antonio."
Jude introduced himself and the others and added. "The guy in the hole is Sherm."

Antonio leaned over the side. "Hello, Mr. Sherm. You don't worry. My cousin Julio bring you a ladder."

Julio turned out to be slender and younger than Antonio, and his wide smile was more reserved. He and Antonio lowered the ladder. "We hold the ladder," said Antonio, "and you come out, Mr. Sherm."

Sherm gathered up the tarp and climbed up with several pairs of hands reaching out to help. Sherm dusted himself off and held out his hand to Julio. "Thanks, friend."

Julio took the big man's hand and turned to Antonio with a quizzical expression. Antonio said something in Spanish, then spoke to Sherman. "Julio don't speak English real good."

Sherm shook the man's hand harder and grinned. "Me neither."

Antonio fingered the tarp. "Very heavy, very strong," he said. "You make a tent?"

"No tent," said Jude. "But we're going to build a boat."

Antonio rubbed his brow and looked confused. "I think I speak English pretty good." His hands made a pleading gesture. "But I think you say you build a boat."

"You heard right," said Jude. He explained about the dory and why they needed it, then Antonio explained to Julio. When Antonio finished translating, Julio replied in Spanish.

Antonio listened carefully and turned to the group. "Julio says birthdays and bicycles are very important for small boys." Antonio put his hand on his cousin's shoulder. "We would like to help."

"Okay," said Sherm. "But we got no money."

"We have no money either, Mr. Sherm," said Antonio. "But we who have so little must share what we have."

With everybody taking turns carrying the heavy canvas, they quickly transported it to the boat. When Antonio saw the dory, his eyes widened, and he whistled softly.

"You very brave, my fren. That boat mostly rotten."

"Not brave," said Jude. "Stupid."

Antonio laughed and kicked the side of the dory.

"Loco, yes. But we cannot always be wise." He turned to Julio and spoke again in Spanish. The younger man started back toward the highway.

Antonio studied the dory and shook his head. "I send my cousin to get tools from the truck and a bottle of Mezcal. That will help us build a strong boat."

"We also need some fishing gear, a light, and bait," said Jude. "Let's divide up the chores and get started."

"Fishing gear's taken care of," said Willy. "I know where there is a box of hooks and a thousand feet of fifty-pound line."

Sometimes, it was better not to ask Willy where he acquired things, and Jude judged this to be one of those times.

"That'll do," he said. "We'll handline the mackerel."

"I'll borrow Vinny's oil lantern," said Lonesome.

"Good. See if you can find something to use as a reflector."

"What about bait?" asked Willy.

"There's mussels all over the breakwater," Jude suggested. "I'll gather some up."

"I'll give you a hand," said Ed.

"You've done your part," Jude urged. "You stay here with Antonio, and help him open that bottle of Mezcal."

"Yes," said Antonio laughing. "I will need help with the Mezcal."

The others departed on their various errands, and Jude made his way out onto the breakwater, a dark and dangerous place at night. The top was flat and walking easy, but eventually, he had to climb down to the high water line to find mussels.

Working almost blind, he pried off thick clusters, leaving behind some of his own skin for the rock crabs to feed on. He bound his booty in his shirt. Their rank odor bothered him more than usual, and so did the cold spray coming up through the stones. He shivered, and the headache thumped behind his eyes. Several times, he coughed hard, and it hurt his chest.

As he approached the bridge, he saw Ed and Sherm unfolding the canvas. Under the bridge, a small fire cast a soft radiance, and Lonesome stood next to it warming her hands. The silky glow highlighted her suntanned face in shades of old ivory and copper.

Ellen was right, he decided. Lonesome did have good bones.

He dumped the mussels by the dory and joined her at the fire. "How did you do?"

She shrugged. "Got the lantern, but Vinny was out of kerosene. He siphoned some diesel out of a big rig parked on the highway. Said it would work but probably smoke a lot."

Julio joined them and handed a bottle to Jude. "Bueno."

Jude looked at the label, all in Spanish. The tawny liquid inside looked hazy, and something dead lay at the bottom. Carefully, Jude sipped. Fire filled his mouth, and his throat felt as if the skin had been stripped off.

He suppressed a cough and passed the bottle to Lonesome. "Muy Bueno."

"What does that mean?" she asked suspiciously.

"Means good." He gave Julio a sly smile. "Very good."

Lonesome turned up the bottle and swallowed. She stood very still, then wheezed slowly as if she'd been struck in the solar plexus. When she tried to speak, the words came out in an unintelligible whoop.

Julio laughed and slapped his leg.

"It's an acquired taste," Jude said. He whacked her back to help her breathe.

"How do you acquire it?" she gasped. "By drinking gasoline?"

Just then, Willy walked into the light, staggering under a diverse burden. Under one arm, he carried a pair of unmatched oars and over his shoulder, a mass of rope. A small bag hung from his free hand.

Jude grabbed the oars. "Good thinking, Willy. We wouldn't go far without these."

Lonesome took the rope. "These look like mooring lines."

"Some of the boats in the marina had two," said Willy. "Thought they could spare one."

With a sigh, Lonesome piled the ropes by the dory. "You really should ask before you borrow things."

"If I did and someone said no, I'd have to steal them. You want me to be a thief?" He handed the small bag to Jude. "Found some nails."

Willy looked at the pile of canvas, and then at the dory. "Gonna be a bitch to measure and cut," he said.

"No need to measure," said Jude. "We'll turn the dory upside down, drape the canvas over it, and cut off the excess."

The method worked well, and before long, the canvas had been cut and folded to fit tightly on the outside of the boat. Using hammers supplied by Antonio, they fastened it to the gunwales with nails. Standing back, Jude surveyed their handiwork.

"She's no Deacon's Masterpiece, but I think she'll do."

He got a puzzled look from Ed. "What the hell is a Deacon's Masterpiece?"

"A poem," said Jude. "About a one horse shay that lasted one hundred years."

Ed shook his head slowly. "Well, this piece of shit won't last a hundred years."

"One night's enough." Jude let his gaze travel over the dory. It wasn't a work of art. The dark canvas stretched and folded over the dory gave it an abstract appearance; a boat drawn by a child — lumpy, out of proportion, and without grace.

"We got a problem," said Lonesome. "No oarlocks,"

Jude picked up a piece of rope, looped it through a side stringer, and tied it off. He shoved an oar through the loop. "Oarlocks."

The Mezcal bottle was almost empty, and Julio's dark face flushed as he held the bottle out to Lonesome. He said something in Spanish.

Antonio laughed. "He wants me to tell the señorita that she can have the last of his Mezcal because she is such a beautiful woman."

Lonesome took the bottle and drank the small amount left in the bottom. She managed to subdue a coughing fit. "Next time warn me about the dead worm." She grinned. "Antonio. Tell your cousin that this cactus-juice whisky has clouded his eyes, but I thank him for the compliment."

When Antonio finished his translation, Julio dropped his eyes and smiled until the sun was rising.

"Time to launch this craft," said Jude.

"Don't we need champagne or somethin' to christen it with?" asked Willy.

"Would you really waste a bottle of wine smashing it on the side of a boat?"

"No. But it's bad mojo to launch a boat without something for luck."

Jude felt his patience slipping. Willy had a streak of superstition that ran deep, and he could be stubborn about his beliefs.

"Wait a minute," Lonesome said. She made her way up into the shadows under the bridge. When she returned, she carried a gallon jug of Red River. "Vinny sent this. He wished us luck. But you are not going to break it on the boat."

"Damn right," said Ed. "Besides, the bottle would probably smash a hole in the side."

"We could just pour a little Red River on it," said Willy.

Ed shuddered. "That might eat the waterproofing off the canvas."

Sherman grabbed the jug. "I fix." He turned up the bottle, drank deeply, and passed it back to Lonesome. "I drink wine." He opened his fly and pissed on the side of their craft. "Then I chrissen."

Willy looked dubious, but he sighed and said. "I guess that'll do."

Grabbing the bow, Ed began dragging the dory toward the water. "Give me a hand."

"Hang on," said Jude. "We can't launch it here. If we row out through the bay, one of the patrol boats will stop us."

Ed straightened up.

"You're right. If they did, they wouldn't waste time writing us a ticket, they'd shoot us."

"There's seven of us," said Jude. "That's enough to carry it across the spit and launch it on the beach behind Surfside."

They turned the dory upside down and carried it like a fourteen-legged bug to the ocean. Just above the surf line, they gently lowered it to the sand and loaded their gear. Sherm stopped and held up a finger.

Jude sighed. "What now, Sherm?"

"Need a name."

"How about Vinny's Luck?" said Lonesome.

"A good name," said Ed. "Cause without a lotta luck, we're probably going to drown."

"Vinny's Luck it is," said Jude. "I'll be the captain, Willy the first mate, Ed the bosun, and Sherm the coxswain."

Sherm screwed up his face. "What mean coxswain?"

"You make sure we go the right direction."

"Okay," said Sherm. "And Lonesome?"

"Most important seafaring job of all, Keeper of the Wine." He pulled the bow around until it pointed out to sea. "Everybody, get on board. Sherm and I will pull it out through the surf. We've done it before."

The Keeper of the Wine was last to board, helped by a drunk, but sincerely gallant Julio. The cousins stood on the shore and raised their hands in salute.

Antonio shouted. "Buenos Amigos, you are very foolish but very, very brave."

Jude and Sherm grabbed each side of the bow and waited for the next wave. The moment water ran under the keel, they dragged the dory into the gentle surf. Crashing through and over the white water, they hauled the dory beyond the breakers where they were pulled on board by the rest of the crew. Ed took up the oars, and the good ship, Vinny's Luck, pulled away on her maiden voyage.

CHAPTER EIGHT

B eyond the surf line, the sea grew tranquil; its colossal power hidden beneath gentle, endless swells. The surface, a vast, wrinkled mirror, stretched out to infinity, reflecting light from a bright, first-quarter moon.

To the north, a jagged line of breakwater stones fractured the brilliant finish, and the sound of water rushing through them sounded like the wail of raging beasts.

After a time, it became apparent that the dory was laboring and not making much progress.

"Jeez," said Willy. "Our wake looks like the track of a drunk snake."

Ed stopped rowing.

"Think you can do better?"

"What's wrong, Ed?" asked Jude.

"These oars Willy stole are too short. I can't get them to dig in."

"Didn't steal them." Willy glared all around. "I borrowed them."

"Don't matter. They're too damn short."

"Try two people rowing side by side," said Jude.

Ed moved to one side. "Might work."

"I help," said Sherm. He squeezed himself in by Ed and took one of the oars. Although the seat was narrow, they each managed to get an oar in the water. Synchronization became a problem. Ed pulled with a slow, deliberate stroke, and Sherm jerked the oar as if he were slamming a car door. The boat swayed and plunged forward in spasmodic bursts but made little headway.

"Let me try," said Willy. But he and Ed fared no better. Ed was the stronger of the two, and the dory tended to move in circles. Frustrated, Willy slammed his oar in the water.

"I can't get the hang of this."

"Give me the oar," said Jude. "It's my turn."

He and Ed managed a collaboration that worked, and the boat moved forward at a better clip.

"Where did you learn to row?" asked Jude. "There aren't any oceans in Arizona."

"Army," said Ed. "Special Forces."

Jude could hear the tension in Ed's voice and dropped the subject. Later, Ed began to tire, and Lonesome tapped him on the shoulder.

"I'll row a while."

Lonesome traded places with Ed and took the oar. She gave Jude a wide grin. "It's just like dancing. You lead, I'll follow." As she positioned the oar, Jude for the first time became aware of her hands. Strong, long fingered, and graceful; they belonged on the strings of a diatonic harp. She noticed his attention. "What's the matter?"

"Nothing," he said. "Just noticed you've got nice hands."

She chuckled lightly. "And you got a nice butt. Now we're even. Let's row."

He and Lonesome fell into immediate harmony, and the gentle gurgle from the bow increased in intensity.

"Damn," said Willy. "You and Lonesome make a good team. We're really moving."

And they were. In perfect cadence, the oars dipped into the water and they pulled. Lift-dip-pull. Lift-dip-pull. The plop and splash of the oars became a hypnotic beat, strong enough to lull the others into silence.

The exercise warmed and loosened his body, and obviously, it produced the same effect on Lonesome. With each stroke, Jude became more aware of her warm, hard-muscled shoulder touching his. Each stroke of the oars brought them into contact, and he found the sensation pleasant. Sweat soaked through her shirt, and her dampness mixed with his own, and somehow that became powerfully erotic.

He was surprised and confused by his body's strong reaction to her. Not that Lonesome was without feminine appeal, her sensuality had simply never touched him before. His unconscious respect for whatever relationship existed between her and Sherman had suppressed his appreciation of her as a woman.

But no longer.

Seated next to him, her heated body in close contact, he could not deny that this was a woman; an intensely desirable one. He was suddenly conscious of her swelling, straining thigh pressed against his own, and a powerful spasm of craving passed through him. Being embarrassed by his own desire was a new sensation for Jude. But lust almost overwhelmed him. He could smell her breath and her body, and he ached to reach out and touch her.

The fact that Lonesome didn't seem to notice his excitement, increased its fervor. He was grateful for the darkness that hid his flushed face.

You're thirty-three years old, he told himself. Stop acting like an overheated adolescent.

Lonesome and Sherman were two of his best friends, and he had no intention of insulting either one by giving in to his own passion.

He took a deep breath and checked their position.

"This is far enough. We're almost to the end of the breakwater."

Ed held up a coil of rope. "I tied all the ropes together for an anchor cable."

Lonesome leaned past Jude to take the line from Ed, and her breast brushed his cheek. Jude dug his fingers into the seat until they penetrated the rotten wood. Grabbing the wine bottle from Willy, he took a swig, hoping to distract his raging hormones.

Desperately, he tried to think of something clever to say, words that he could hide behind. Nothing. His mind was blank.

Lonesome tied the line to a chunk of concrete brought along to serve as an anchor. She dropped it over the side and passed the free end to Willy to tie off at the bow. As she straightened, she put her hand on Jude's shoulder, and he shivered involuntarily. In the darkness, she peered at his face.

"Are you all right?"

"Yeah, I'm fine." He was amazed at how lucid and clever his response sounded.

Lonesome placed the back of her fingers on his cheek. "You feel like you've got a fever."

"Just the exercise," he said. "Let's catch some mackerel."

Willy cut them each a length of line and tied a hook on the end. Jude began opening mussels, and Lonesome lit the lantern. Vinny's prediction that the diesel fuel would smoke proved correct. Nevertheless, it cast sufficient light for their purpose. Mackerel tended to gather around any source of radiance, and Jude doubted they cared whether it was generated by a smoky diesel lantern or a full moon. He rigged an oar to hold the lantern over the water and began to bait their hooks.

For an hour, nothing happened. Then the pool of luminescence, cast by the lantern, began to fill with small darting creatures, too small to make out their species. When the activity became frenetic, larger forms, sleek and decisive, flashed through the light.

"Got one," yelled Willy.

He yanked aboard a flopping, foot-long mackerel. It lay in the bottom of the boat, its mottled gunmetal body writhing. As if it were a signal, everyone was hooked up.

At first, each catch was greeted with whoops and cheers, but before long, it became just another piece of work. Arms ached with the constant motion, hand lines slashed into fingers, and the fish slime caused the cuts to burn and itch. In an hour, the bottom of the boat was evenly covered by the small fish.

"How much do you think we've got?" asked Ed.

"About fifty pounds," said Jude. "We'll need at least another hundred and fifty."

The hookups slacked off for a while, and they passed the   time sipping Red River and talking. Jude pushed his hook through a piece of tough bait and dropped it over the side.

"Ed, you remember your first bicycle?"

For a moment, Ed stared into the distance.

"Hell yeah. It was red with chrome fenders. Dad brought it home on my ninth birthday. Some of the kids on the reservation couldn't afford bikes, so everybody got to ride mine."

"I didn't know you lived on a reservation," said Willy.

"For a few years. My dad's full-blooded Apache. Mom was from Mexico. When she died, dad moved us all back on the reservation. I didn't leave until I was drafted."

A dreamy expression settled on Sherman's broad face. "Christmas," he said softly. "Some things I don't remember too good. But remember my first bike. Had a shiny little bell." He sighed. "Can't drive no more. Maybe someday I buy me nuther bicycle." He laughed, a husky deep sound of real humor. "Saw Lonesome ride once. She make bike do tricks."

"Where did you learn to do trick stuff, Lonesome?" asked Willy.

"From a bike messenger that lived next door. Everybody called him Lightning Joe." Her expression turned misty. "Dad didn't want me to have a bike. He wanted me to concentrate on my . . ." She cleared her throat and changed tack. "Mom decided if I wanted a bike, I could have one. It was great. Lightning Joe taught me to do tricks all the boys on the block envied." She gave Jude a grin. "I'll bet you built your first bike out of junk parts."

"Damn, Lonesome. Do you read minds or did I tell you that story?"

"Neither," she said. "Just sounded like something you'd do."

With a slow shake of his head, Jude spoke. "My parents were too poor to buy me one. Took all summer crawling through junk heaps and buying broken down bikes. Had to mow lawns for the money to buy parts and paint. Don't remember why, but I picked grass-green." He laughed. "It was the ugliest bicycle in the neighborhood, but it was also the fastest. I did love that bike."

"How about you, Willy?" asked Lonesome.

Willy looked away. "I wasn't allowed to ride one." He pulled in his line and rebaited. "It would be kinda nice if little Toby remembered us as the ones who bought him his first bike."

"Yes," said Jude. "That would be a good thing."

The mackerel began to bite again, and for the time, the fishermen concentrated on baiting hooks and unhooking fish.

Sometime after midnight, a haze descended, slowly closing the world in around the five friends in their small, rickety boat. It thickened slowly with unhurried malevolence into a dense, sound-smothering fog. Their realm shrunk to a tiny, arms-length microcosm, lurid in the flickering lantern light and bounded by soft, impenetrable mist. In the distance, a foghorn began to mourn.

Willy looked frightened. "How are we going to know which way to go ashore?"

"Listen," said Jude.

"For what?" Ed held his hand to his ear.

"Waves on the breakwater," said Jude. "Hear them?"

"Yeah, so what?"

"When we're ready to leave, we put that sound to our left and keep it there."

"I don't know," Willy said dubiously.

Jude laughed. "Don't worry, Odin will take care of us."

Ed unhooked a mackerel and tossed it on the growing pile. "Who the hell is Odin?"

"The Norsemen's chief god, the God of the Sea."

"You mean like Neptune?" asked Willy.

"Neptune is Roman, Odin is a Viking god."

Shaking his head, Ed muttered, "Goddamn it, Jude, nobody should know as much shit as you do."

"How you learn things, Jude?" asked Sherman.

"He reads," said Willy. "Reads every damn thing he can lay his hands on. Even the labels on ketchup bottles."

Sherm gave Jude an earnest look. "Maybe someday you teach me to read?"

"You bet."

For hours, they caught fish and drank wine. Isolated from and unconstrained by traditional morality, they nevertheless lived by a code as stringent as anything formulated by Hammurabi. If a personal question was met with reluctance or pain, it was immediately abandoned. Each one was accepted and valued for what they were now, not what they might have the potential to become. Respect was a word they never used but a concept they practiced assiduously.

After a time, lack of sleep began to catch up to the fishermen. Everyone was yawning, and Sherman's head nodded spasmodically.

"Anybody got a watch?" asked Jude.

No one responded. Time wasn't ordinarily an important factor in their lives, watches were useless baubles.

Willy rubbed his face and stretched. "Must be close to dawn. The fish have stopped biting."

Ed toed the pile of mackerel. "How much you think we've got?"

"Could be enough," said Jude. "Even if it isn't, I think it's all we're going to get tonight."

"Hal opens the baitshop at six," said Lonesome.

Jude kicked Sherman's foot. Sherm snorted, sat up, and rubbed his eyes.

"Get as far forward as you can and listen for the breakwater," instructed Jude. "Keep your arm pointed toward it so Lonesome and I will know which way to row."

While Sherman shifted positions, Ed pulled up the anchor. Willy held the lantern uncertainly.

"Maybe we should leave this lit, in case we meet another boat."

"Be serious." Ed laughed wryly. "No one else is stupid enough to be out here in this fog."

"Besides," said Jude. "If we dropped that thing and it started a fire . . ."

"Right," said Willy. "A shitty way to cook mackerel."

Jude turned to Lonesome. "Ready?"

"At your command, Captain."

"Make for shore. Flank speed."

It quickly became apparent that any speed would be difficult. Weighted down with fish, the dory moved sluggishly and only with great effort. Even the gentle swells caused it to groan alarmingly. Jude began to wonder how they were going to get it through the surf in one piece.

"Slow and easy," he said to Lonesome. She matched his deliberate pace. "Sherm, can you hear the surfline yet?"

Sherman listened intently and shook his head.

Just as Jude put his oar back into the water, a mackerel gave its tail one final flip and slid down the heap. Slowly, a slimy avalanche commenced as the pile of fish slid against the side of the dory. The crew shifted to compensate, and a loud crack came from somewhere.

No one moved. For a while, there was no other sound, then quietly but distinctly came the gurgle of water.

"Can anybody see where it's coming from?" asked Jude.

"Can't see anything with the bottom a foot deep in mackerel," Willy said.

Ed sat on the stern seat, tension lines creasing his forehead. "This Odin, you mentioned. You think he might help us out?"

"Don't know," said Jude. "Anyone here besides me got any Viking blood?"

"Strictly Irish," said Willy.

"Don't know," Sherm added.

"Me neither." Lonesome looked vaguely disappointed.

Ed shook his head. "Hell, I'm half Apache, remember. Our gods don't even know there is a damned ocean."

Jude sighed. "Guess it's up to me." He shook his clenched fist at the sky. "Odin you red-bearded shithead. Give us a hand here."

Ed looked up toward the dark fogged over sky. "That wasn't exactly what I had in mind."

Sherm reached under the bow seat and took out a rusty five-pound coffee can. He handed it to Ed. "Bailing is better'n prayin."

Jude dipped his oar into the water. "Come on Lonesome, it's row or swim."

Although they managed to get the dory moving, it was slow and exhausting. The fish were beginning to float, and Ed swore as he bailed faster. Willy began to dip out water with his cupped palms.

The water was nearly to Jude's ankle. "The surf, Sherm, can you hear it?"

"Think so—maybe. But long way off."

Water lapped over Jude's calf. His chest heaved painfully as he dug in the oars and tried to keep the dory moving. Beside him, he could hear Lonesome gasping, but gamely, she kept her oar moving.

Ed was bailing frantically, generating an almost steady stream of water, but it wasn't enough. Vinny's Luck was running out.

Jude stopped rowing. "This isn't going to work. Everybody out of the boat except Ed."

"What good's that going to do?" asked Ed.

"The dory's made of wood. It will float if it's not carrying too much of a load. We've got to save those mackerel." He eased himself over the side. Lonesome followed. They hung on to the gunwale, now just a few inches out of the water. Willy dived off, and Sherman simply fell in.

"I think it's working." Ed sounded relieved. "The boat's nearly full, but it's stopped sinking."

Hanging on with one hand, Willy wiped water from his face. "How are we going to get it to shore."

Sherman swam around the boat and stopped next to Jude. "You and me. Tie ropes and we pull it."

"Might work," said Jude. He studied the dory. A small, wooden Samson post was set in the bow plate. "Just like an old pair of mules in a harness."

"Hard job. Real hard." Sherm grinned. "One mule not enough."

"Ed, can you find the ropes?"

Ed leaned over. They heard a splash, and Ed groaned. "Jeez, the water's all slimy." He untangled the lines and passed two to Jude.

They were mooring lines with a loop spliced in one end.

"Tie the free end around your waist," Jude ordered. When he and Sherman were harnessed, he dropped the loops over the Samson post.

Lonesome swam to his side. "I'm a good swimmer. I can help."

Shaking his head, Jude put his hand on her shoulder and lowered his voice. "You make sure Ed gets to shore."

She gave him a strange look and nodded.

"Willy. You're the scout. Swim just in front of me and Sherm and listen for the surf. We'll follow you." He turned to Sherm. "Ready?"

"Ready." Sherm turned and began to swim.

When the rope pulled tight, Jude knew he was in for a painful experience. The rope bit savagely into his hip bones, and he was forced to tuck his shirt under it. At first, he wasn't even sure the dory was moving, but he heard Willy shout.

"It's moving! Goddamn, it's moving!"

After an eternity, his shoulders began to ache, and his breath came in a painful wheeze between each stroke. Sherm swam like a machine — powerfully, tirelessly.

Another eternity passed, and he remembered mere pain with fondness. The rope wore through his shirt, and a ring of raw skin around his waist felt scalded. Blinding, white-hot agony burned in every joint and muscle.

He could hear Sherm gasping now and knew if they didn't reach shore soon, they would lose the dory — and the mackerel. Below the rope, his waist felt numb, and with each breath, he coughed cold, salty water from his lungs. He turned to tell Sherman that he could go no farther, when suddenly his knees slammed into something. Water filled his mouth; he gagged, and a wave broke over him.

Wave. He was in the surf.

Struggling to his feet, he looked over to see Sherman also trying to stand. Together, they strained in their harness and, aided by the next incoming breaker, the dory slid up on the beach.

Jude collapsed and fell face first into the wet sand. After a few minutes, his breathing steadied, and he turned his head. Sherm lay next to him, gasping, his beard clotted with sand. The big man reached out and, lying exhausted in the sand, they shook hands.

Sherm gave him a weak grin. "Jude, you one damn fine mule."

CHAPTER NINE

A frothy comber washed over Jude's legs and left a ring of foam on his thighs. He rolled over on his side and saw the dory lying broken and shapeless just inside the farthest advance of the surf.

Each new wave poured water into the wrecked hull.

Lonesome began tearing the canvas from the dory's frame, and Ed pitched in to help. Vaguely, Jude wondered why.

"Hurry," Lonesome said. "We got to get the mackerel out of the water or we'll lose them."

Alarmed, Jude tried to scramble to his feet, but his head felt full and heavy, and the world spun out of control. A strong arm caught him as he fell.

"Sit," said Sherm. "I help Lonesome."

Weak and shaky, Jude lowered himself to the sand and placed his head on his knees. A wave of nausea overcame him, and he retched, expelling a gout of seawater. After a while, he washed his face in the cool surf and felt better. Raising his head, he saw the others tossing mackerel from the wrecked dory onto the canvas. He stood up, and this time, although wobbly, he managed to stay upright.

Ed saw him approaching. "We lost a few, Jude."

Lonesome glanced over her shoulder and abruptly turned to look again. "You're really pale."

"I'm all right. Just swallowed too much of the damned ocean." The pile of salvaged fish looked considerably smaller than the original catch. "Hope there's enough left."

Gathering the corners of the canvas, they tied them with the remaining rope. The resulting bundle was heavy, unwieldy, and required all of them to carry.

"It's a good thing we don't have to haul this very far," Willy grumbled.

By the time they reached the bait shop, they were all stumbling with fatigue. They dropped their slimy burden near the door and fell in exhausted heaps wherever they stood.

The bait shop was a concrete block cube, unplastered, unpainted, and without any decorative refinement whatsoever. The front door sat dead center with large windows on either side. Iron grillwork protected the windows, and inside, a dim light burned to foil potential thieves. Over the door, a small wooden sign proclaimed it as Hal's Bait Shop.

Ed leaned back against the side of the building. "I'm so damned hungry, I could eat a boiled rock."

"All I want is sleep," said Lonesome. She tried to pull her wet hair back into a ponytail but finally gave up.

The fog thinned, and through the filmy gauze, Jude could see a silver veil of light creeping up from the east. Sherman began to snore, and although Willy's eyes remained open, he had either gone to sleep or died.

A combination of wet clothes and cool air chilled Jude to the bone, and spasms in his jaw muscles forced him to clench his teeth to keep them from chattering. To make his torture more exquisite, each time he moved, the rope burns on his hips felt as if a hot iron seared his flesh. But eventually, even profound discomfort would not keep sleep at bay, and he found himself in a hazy state halfway between asleep and awake. The sights and sounds around him registered on his mind, but stirred no response.

The staccato rattle of an engine blasting through a broken muffler jolted him fully awake. A vehicle turned into the side street from Pacific Coast Highway, its headlights forming big, yellow halos in the haze. When it came closer, Jude recognized Hal's old pickup.

When the truck pulled in to the parking lot, the lights swept across them. Hal unfolded his bony frame from the truck, slowly and suspiciously.

"What the hell do you bunch of bums want?" He walked toward them with a jerky, awkward gait that reminded Jude of a spastic stork.

"We've got some mackerel," said Jude.

Hal stopped and regarded them with his flat, muddy brown eyes. The sallow, open-pored skin on his gaunt cheeks creased as he grinned, exposing teeth as rotten and crooked as a collapsing fence. No one, however, mistook that terrible smirk for an expression of humor.

It was, Jude thought, a face that would feel at home in a lynch mob.

"What makes you think I'll buy anything from the likes of you?" asked Hal.

Jude clamped down on his temper. "You've got a sign out front."

Hal shrugged and toed the tarp. "So what?" His sly expression told Jude to be wary.

"You want them or not," Jude snapped. "If you don't, we'll dump them in the bay."

Hal stepped back and put his hands on his hips. "Open it up."

Ed and Willy untied the ropes and rolled the canvas open. Jude could see the greed in Hal's gaze.

"Give you forty cents a pound," Hal bargained.

"The sign says fifty," said Willy.

"Maybe it does," Hal pointed to his chest with his thumb, "but I say forty."

"Look," said Jude. "We're trying to buy little Toby a bicycle for his birthday."

Hal hooted and slapped his leg. "You bunch of bums trying to be boy scouts or somethin'? Don't bullshit me. It's forty cents a pound. Take it or leave it."

Again, Jude smothered an angry response. Ed stood up slowly, an ugly expression pulling his face taut. Lonesome lay her hand on Willy's arm, and he inched closer. Ed could be dangerous if sufficiently aroused, and a physical confrontation would spoil whatever chance they had of selling the mackerel. Had the circumstances been otherwise, Jude would have walked away and dumped the mackerel in the bay. But the money was for Toby.

He swallowed his pride. "All right. If it's cash."

"It'll be cash," said Hal. "But you assholes will load this slimy mess into my freezer for me." He leaned forward, his eyes glittering with sly triumph. "Or you get nothing."

Chuckling at his mastery, Hal opened his shop. He pointed to a big horizontal freezer along the back wall.

"Put them on the right side and stack them careful. I already got two hundred pounds of squid in there." He pointed to a stack of dirty wooden boxes. "Use those to haul the fish in, and I'll weigh them."

They spent the next hour carrying in the mackerel, weighing them and stacking them in the freezer. Hal tallied up the amounts. "A hundred and seventy-six pounds. That comes to seventy dollars and forty cents, except I ain't givin' you the forty cents cause I ain't got no change."

"Goddamn it, Hal. We need a hundred dollars."

"I don't give a shit what you need. Seventy dollars is what you get." Hal pulled a wad of bills from his pocket and counted out the money, slapping each bill on the counter.

Carefully, bill by bill, Jude recounted. From the corner of his eye he saw Willy slip into the back of the room.

"What's the matter? You don't trust me?" Hal asked.

Jude leaned close and could smell the man's foul breath. "No. I don't." He noticed Willy quietly rejoin them. "You're a human cockroach, Hal, and someday I'm going to step on you." Jude stuffed the bills in his pocket.

Hal stood open mouthed but showed enough wisdom to keep his council.

"Come on," Jude said to the others. "Let's go over to the Shack. Vinny will be open by now."

"Just like I figured," Hal muttered as they walked away. "Going to get drunk and do whatever else you bums do."

Ed started to turn back toward Hal, but Jude stopped him. "He really isn't worth it."

Willy took Ed's arm.

"Come on. There's other ways of dealing with an asshole like Hal."

Jude wondered what Willy's sly expression meant.

Vinny stood outside the Shack shaking down a huge ring of keys. His eyes widened when he saw them drawing near. "Good God. You guys look like you've spent the night in a sewer." He selected a key and fitted it in the door.

"A sewer would have been more comfortable," said Jude.

"Come on in," said Vinny. "I'll make a pot of coffee."

Inside, the air was stuffy and filled with the odor of ancient tobacco smoke. From the far corner, Hoocher, Vinny's old basset hound, crawled out of his cardboard box and greeted them with a wagging tail.

Hoocher was past his prime and tended to be fat, primarily because his diet consisted mainly of popcorn and jerky sticks, washed down with an occasional dollop of warm wine. He was Vinny's night watchman, and although a gentle, loving creature when Vinny was present, he took his job seriously. One intruder had underestimated the old hound's resolve and broke in through one of the Shack's primitive windows. After encountering Hoocher, the man had left behind a shoe, a torn trouser leg, and a substantial puddle of piss.

Vinny leaned precariously on his crutch and patted the dog's head. "Go on outside and do your business, old fella. I'll feed you when you come back."

Hoocher took his time, waddling from one paw to the other, giving everyone a friendly sniff before making his way out and down the steps.

Vinny set up his percolator and started coffee while the rest of the group slumped around the bar. "You guys get any mackerel?"

"Not enough," said Jude.

Vinny gave him a sad look. "Wish I could help, Jude." His expression was pleading. "When Hoocher got hit by that truck, you guys all pitched in and helped pay his vet bill. But you know I got to send my ex-wife all my money. If I don't, she won't let me visit my little girls."

Lonesome leaned across the bar and wrapped Vinny in her arms, hugging him ferociously.

"You've got nothing to apologize for, Vinny."

"That's right," Ed added. "You're one of the few decent people I know."

Vinny turned away and busied himself pouring coffee.

"You guys look hungry." He opened a small refrigerator next to the cash register and took out a loaf of bread, a quart of orange marmalade, and a gallon of peanut butter. He placed them on the bar. "Help yourself."

Everyone made their sandwiches quietly, almost reverently. To be allowed to share Vinny's peanut butter was the highest honor he ever accorded anyone. He poured mugs of coffee, sipped his own, and sighed with satisfaction. "A little weak, but not bad."

"Weak," said Willy. "This stuff would run a diesel engine."

"Yeah," said Vinny, "but good coffee would blow it up." He moved to the cash register and picked up a note on the top. "By the way, Willy, last night after you left someone called here for you." He squinted at the note. "Name was Cragen."

"Shit." Willy looked pale. "What did he want?"

"Said he was coming down here today to talk to you."

"Who's Cragen?" asked Ed.

"My uncle," said Willy. "Probably wants to try and screw me out of my inheritance."

"Maybe he loan you money?" said Sherm.

Willy's answer was a derisive snort. "He wouldn't piss on me if I was on fire."

"I've met Cragen," said Jude. "He's definitely not the answer to our problem."

"How much do you need?" asked Vinny.

"Another thirty dollars." Jude looked at the calendar, but it was three years old and on the wrong month. He turned to Vinny. "What day is it?"

He got a startled look from Vinny. "Saturday."

"Saturday's a good day for pool hustling, Willy."

"Good idea," said Ed. "Willy never loses."

That drew a disgusted look from Willy.

"All the locals know me. Who the hell am I going to hustle?"

Carefully, Vinny eased himself into his chair behind the bar. "There's a bunch of rich college kids moved into Surfside. They've been hanging out at Barny's, and college kids always think they're pretty good pool players."

"The problem," said Jude, "would be getting Willy into Barny's."

Barny's, in spite of its pedestrian appellation, was a high class watering hole that catered to upper class and above. Patrons of the Shack were not welcome there.

"True," said Vinny. "They wouldn't let you in there dressed like that."

"Got a good pair of pants," said Willy. "But all my shirts are pretty raggedy."

"I've a white turtleneck," Lonesome offered. "That college crowd would probably think that was cool."

Willy looked down at his bare feet. "They won't let me in without shoes."

"Maybe we could paint your feet black," Ed suggested.

"Not funny," said Lonesome.

"Wait now," said Vinny. "I got a pair of white shoes someone left in the motel. They're kinda beat up, but we could dye them or something."

"Go get your clean pants," said Jude. "We'll take care of the shoes."

"I'm going to need Sherm as a bodyguard. Even college kids can get pretty mean if they think they've been hustled."

A minor panic ensued. Vinny held up his hand for quiet. "My clothes will fit Sherm, except for the pants."

And so, Sherm was outfitted in a black broadcloth jacket and white shirt. Pants proved a dilemma. The cuffs had to be turned under and pinned with twelve inches of waistband gathered and held in the back. But the jacket covered the misfit, and everyone agreed, Sherm looked like a Mafia hit man.

While Willy was gone, Jude retrieved the shoes from the motel storage room. They were plain white loafers, the kind worn by waitresses and dental technicians. Although they were about the right size, white would be noticed, and Willy needed to attract as little attention as possible.

"Don't have any black dye or shoe polish," said Vinny.

Ed brushed dust off one of the shoes. "Maybe we could rub some charcoal on them."

"Your first idea was best," said Jude. "We need black paint."

"Check my storage shed out back," said Vinny. "I think there might be some."

Ed returned in a few minutes carrying a quart can with black dribbles of dried paint on the side. Jude fashioned a brush from a piece of paper towel and painted the shoes. He stood back and admired his handywork. "They'll be all right until that paint hardens enough to crack."

Willy returned wearing clean khaki pants and Lonesome's turtleneck. The shoes turned out to be a size too large, but stuffed with paper, Willy decided he could wear them.

"Not bad," said Jude. "With a haircut, you'd pass for a real person."

"Give me a break, Jude." He checked his appearance in a small mirror over the cash register. "Hustling isn't much fun when you really need the money."

"How much seed money do you need?" asked Jude.

"Ten's enough for college kids, and I don't intend to tangle with another hustler."

Jude took a ten dollar bill from the mackerel money. "We're counting on you."

Willy stuffed the bill in his pocket. "Don't get your hopes up too high. This will probably be nickel and dime stuff." He took Sherm's arm. "On our way to Barny's, you can practice your menacing look."

"Okay," said Sherm. "What means menacing?"

As the two men walked away, Ed spoke. "I think I'll go to the marina. Might get a little work scraping barnacles."

Jude turned to Lonesome. "How do you feel about a car wash."

She grinned. "We'll need soap."

"Always one more problem," said Jude.

CHAPTER TEN

One of the first lessons Jude had learned about a life of simplicity and poverty is that the niceties of civilization could sometimes be hard to come by. At this moment, soap became one of those difficulties. Vinny had only a tiny piece in his shower, and nothing at all in the Shack's toilets.

He and Lonesome stood outside while pondering the problem. Lonesome gave him a puzzled look. "You ever wonder who invented soap?"

"Wasn't really invented. It was discovered, and like most of mankind's discoveries, they stumbled over it."

"How would you discover soap?"

"Dumb luck. Ancient men sacrificed animals to their gods, and when fat from slaughtered animals mixed with potash left by the sacrificial fires, the product was soap. Mankind discovered soap, and womankind made him learn to use it."

She laughed. "Ed's right. You know way too much shit for your own good." She tapped him on the skull. "And it doesn't help us find soap right now."

Jude looked up and down the street. Sunrise had begun to dissipate the fog and add a touch of warmth to the air. Across the highway, the liquor store lights were still out. It wouldn't open until ten, nor would the small family market just down the street.

"Little Toby is supposed to be home by noon. We don't have time to walk to the all-night market in Seal Beach."

"We can't wash cars without soap," said Lonesome.

"Come on, lady friend. I'm all out of ideas."

She cocked her head quizzically. "You never called me lady before."

A rush of heat to his face caused him to look away. Last night's hormone rampage had changed his attitude toward Lonesome more than he cared to admit, and this new sensibility was seeping into everything he said. It was definitely time to change the subject.

"Soap, Lonesome. Concentrate on soap."

"How about the powdered stuff in the gas station bathroom?"

For a moment, he thought about it. "It's got pumice in it. We'd scratch off a lot a paint."

"How about we filter the pumice out through an old T-shirt?"

"Might work," said Jude. "But they keep the bathroom locked unless you buy gas."

"The guys will let me in." Again, she gave him that enigmatic smile. "Because I'm a lady."

Jude felt as if he were engaged in some sort of competition and only Lonesome knew the rules. But he did know that he was down on points. "Okay. I'm game."

"Give me your shirt," she said. "It's all tore up anyway."

He shucked out of the shirt, and Lonesome's face froze.

"What's the matter?" Following her gaze, he looked down. Across each hip ran a long welt, raw and oozing. "Just rope burn."

She smacked his arm, but gently. "Stop being so damned macho. As soon as the store opens, we're using some of that money to buy ointment."

This is no time to argue, he thought. He tried a diversion. "Can we go get the soap now?"

He waited across the highway while Lonesome smiled at the attendant and gestured to the bathroom. The young man said something to Lonesome, they both laughed, and he handed her a ring of keys. She returned in a few minutes bearing his old T-shirt full of powdered hand soap.

They scrounged a bucket from behind the restaurant and filled it with water. The hand soap, even after being filtered, turned the water milky and exuded a harsh, medicinal odor.

A hundred yards south of the Shack lay a narrow strip of land, unused except as parking for an occasional big rig. Vinny provided them with a leaky garden hose to rinse the cars, and they connected it to a hose bib outside the motel. Jude used a chunk of charcoal from the barbecue to letter a sign on the side of a cast off cardboard box.

Beach Bum Car Wash.
One Dollar.

"A dollar's not very much," said Lonesome.

"I know," said Jude. "But if we charge more, we might not get anyone to stop."

They sat down in the shade of a small billboard, the only shade for half a mile. While they waited, Bad Kitty, the tomcat that lived under the Shack, sauntered by, keeping a wary eye on them. Bad Kitty was steel gray with scattered, random patterns of black, accentuated here and there by an old combat scar. He had the disposition of a wood chipper and the sudden, vicious temper of a chain saw. The ten-pound lean, battlewise carnivore accepted neither affection nor food from anyone. Every morsel he ate was either stolen or scavenged, and Bad Kitty liked it that way.

The cat sniffed the bucket of soapy water, flipped his tail into the air, and moved on. At the very edge of the shade, as far from Jude and Lonesome as possible, he flopped down and began to clean his scraggly fur.

"Bad Kitty is friendlier than usual," said Lonesome.

"Real mellow. Must have stolen a pickled egg from Vinny again."

Bad Kitty stopped his grooming and peered intently at a thin, sharp-boned woman emerging from the shadows of a roadside culvert. She climbed up onto the highway shoulder and moved away with a peculiar and instantly recognizable stride. Each step began by pushing her bony hip forward, then allowing her foot to strike the earth as flat as the tread of an elephant, sending little squirts of dust from beneath her worn shoes.

"Looks like Gray Lady's headed for Old Dan's," said Jude.

"She's there every morning," said Lonesome. "But she never goes inside."

"She'll turn into the alley," said Jude. "Pedro, the bus boy, sneaks food out for her and hides it in the dumpster."

They watched as she made her way past the bait shop, looking neither left nor right. No one knew her real name. She had acquired the title of Gray Lady from the stark, gray sheath-dress she invariably wore. Gray, however, described her physical essence, gray hair, gray eyes, even skin the texture and color of ancient limestone.

There had been some speculation that the dress was a uniform issued by a mental institution and that Gray Lady was a runaway. But she spoke to no one, bothered no one, and asked for nothing. In Sunset Beach, those virtues were considered sufficient to grant one sainthood. She was left alone.

Just as Jude predicted, Gray Lady turned into the alley and disappeared from view.

Lonesome let her gaze roam up and down the highway. "Not much business yet."

"You're stating the obvious," said Jude.

A hurt expression crossed her face. "You sound awful prickly."

"I am," he said. "But there's no excuse for snapping at you." He remembered Toby's shy smile, and a sudden aching knot of emotion almost closed his throat. "I'm sorry, Lonesome. This thing is eating at me."

She put her hand lightly on his arm. "I know it is, Jude. I understand." A sly, mischievous grin showed her even teeth. "But if you do it again, I'll beat the shit outta you."

He laughed and started to put his arm around her shoulder in a show of affection but thought better of it. Touching her had taken on a new significance, and he no longer trusted his body in contact with hers. Besides, even with stringy hair and tattered, salt-stained clothes, she managed to maintain a strong aura of femininity.

Lonesome studied his face. "All of us are set on getting that bicycle for Toby, but I've never seen you this intense about anything."

"I don't understand either," said Jude. "It's something I have to do."

"Sherm says Toby reminds him of his own little boy."

"I didn't know Sherm had any kids."

"Two, a boy and a girl." She watched Bad Kitty scratch his back by rolling in the dirt. "Did you know Sherm gets a disability check every month?"

"No. He never mentioned it, and he never has any money."

"He doesn't cash it. Just signs it and I mail it to his ex-wife."

"For the kids?"

She nodded.

"After the accident, Sherm couldn't speak at all for a while. His wife freaked out, couldn't handle it, so she divorced him. Sherm still can't speak very well, but he feels things—deeply. He knew he'd be a drag on his family, so he packed a few clothes and took off."

"I should be surprised," said Jude. "I'm not. That's the kind of thing he'd do." He gave Lonesome a grin. "But I was surprised to see you belly dance."

A shadow fell over her eyes, and she looked away. "Belly dancing was just for fun, but ballet was once my whole life."

"I didn't intend to pry, Lonesome."

She turned and leaned her shoulder on the sign so she could face him. "If there's anything I'm sure of, Jude, it's that you would never snoop around in someone else's life." She added more softly. "Or let anyone snoop into yours."

She rested her head on the sign, and for a moment, Jude thought she might be asleep. Weariness had deepened the shadows on her face, but it was a countenance with enough character to withstand the ravages of exhaustion. When she spoke, it was soft, and he had to strain to hear.

"My father wanted me to be a ballerina from the moment I could walk."

"Is that what you wanted?"

She opened her eyes. "I thought so then. For years, I trained and studied, and I was pretty good. By the time I finished college, my instructor thought I was ready for the big time. To prove it, he married me."

"Sounds a little cold."

"It seemed like love at the time. With both Alfred and my father pushing me, I became an excellent dancer. But excellence isn't enough in dance. You have to be great, and I gradually realized that I never would be."

"You gave it up?"

"Not quite that simple. A kid on a skate board ran into me in a crosswalk. I hit the pavement so hard, my back broke in three places. The doctors didn't think I'd ever walk again."

"You proved them wrong."

"Walk yes, but dance . . ." She shook her head.

"Disappointed?"

"It was tough at first. I went back to school and got a teaching credential. But Alfred decided that if I couldn't dance, I couldn't be his wife. Sherm and I have that much in common. We're both rejects."

"Alfred sounds like an asshole."

She grinned. "He is." The smile faded. "But my father did the most damage. After mom died, he became even more obsessed. He just wouldn't accept the fact that I would never be a ballerina. He dragged me from one rehab clinic to another, trying to find someone that could fix his broken dancer."

"When's the last time you talked to your dad?"

"It's been more than five years." Leaning back, she closed her eyes. "I just got tired of not being what everybody else wanted me to be." Her voice was now a little more than a whisper. "Last night when I tried to dance and couldn't, it hurt, but it was just physical pain. I found I didn't really care anymore."

Her voice trailed off, and this time, Jude could see her falling asleep. His gut burned with disgust and anger. That someone would use up and discard such a decent human being, infuriated him. He'd known Lonesome for a couple of years, and she'd never spoken of her life before coming to Sunset Beach. He wondered if even Sherman knew her story.

Lonesome's nap wasn't destined to last long. Their first customers, a van load of wealthy teenagers, were impressed at having their vehicle washed by real beach bums. The driver, a pubescent girl wearing a bikini that covered approximately three square inches of flesh, giggled.

"This is absolutely, totally cool." She left an extra dollar as a tip.

As the van pulled out, a big white Mercedes pulled in.

"Maybe this is going to work out," said Lonesome.

The driver's side door opened, and a young man exited. Taller than Jude and fashionably slender, he wore expensive clothes that were cut to look stylishly sloppy. In one hand he carried a black, leather organizer as if it had been grafted to his palm.

Yuppie, thought Jude. The hair on the back of his neck stood up like the hackles on a mongoose confronting a cobra.

The yuppie strutted around the car toward them, a contemptuous smile flashing several thousand dollars worth of cosmetic dentistry.

"How much to wash the tires and wheels and grill? I don't want the rest of the car touched."

"One dollar," said Jude.

Again the contemptuous smile. "You charge full pay for half a job? That doesn't sound right."

"It's one dollar whether I wash the hood ornament or the whole damn car," said Jude.

The yuppie barked a laugh as if he'd won a point. "All right. Do it." He turned to the car where another man sat in the passenger side. "Come on, Gill. Let's get a beer while the beach bums wash my tires."

The other man turned out to be taller than the yuppie, with a soft, irresolute expression. He held his brown leather organizer awkwardly, and his clothes looked merely expensive.

"Where can we get a cold beer," snapped the yuppie.

"Across the street at the Marina restaurant."

When the two men were gone, Lonesome muttered. "What a jerk."

"Almost makes Hal look like a nice guy," said Jude.

"Why didn't you send him to the Shack? Vinny could use the business."

"If he smart mouthed Vinny, he'd get his head smacked, and then we might not get our dollar."

They cleaned the tires and rims and scrubbed bug guts off the grill. When it was finished, everything sparkled. They waited a half hour for the two men to return.

"Get in the car, Gill," said the yuppie. He walked around the car inspecting their work carefully. With a phony look of surprise, he patted his pocket. "My wallet's in the car. Hang on. I'll get it." He climbed into the car and started the engine. Gravel spurted from the rear tires as he accelerated away. Jude could see the man's face in the rear-view mirror, laughing.

Using the charcoal, Jude wrote the Mercedes' license number on the box and held it up for the yuppie to see.

"That sick son of a bitch," Lonesome snarled. "Are you going to call the cops?"

"Won't do any good," said Jude.

She gave him an odd look. "Why did you write down the number?"

"He knows I've got his license number, but he doesn't know I don't intend to turn him in. When he thinks about it, he'll worry a little."

"I'd rather kick him in the balls," said Lonesome.

"I have got to remember not to piss you off." Jude set down the box and found himself a place in the shade.

Lonesome joined him and sighed as she settled. She stared down the highway in the direction the Mercedes had disappeared. "Every year, there are more people like him," she said.

"Scary, isn't it? They see themselves as wolves, predators. Truth is, they're rats sniffing around in dark places where the real wolves won't notice them."

"Like the rich guy?"

"Yes," said Jude. "The rich guy is definitely a wolf. He's probably used up and burned out a hundred ambitious, cold-blooded bastards like the yuppie."

Lonesome looked distant and introspective. "Where do we fit in, Jude?"

"I hope—truly hope, we are the human beings."

"That would be enough," she said and leaned back against the sign. Looking over Jude's shoulder, she squinted. "Gray Lady's coming this way."

Jude turned his head and saw the woman walking toward them, her eye focused on the ground straight ahead. About a hundred feet from them, she spied Jude and stopped. For a moment, she stared at him, then dropped her eyes and contemplated the dust at her feet. She seemed to be arguing with herself. Abruptly, she moved forward with the same peculiar gait, veering her steps in his direction.

Implacably, her advance continued until she was just inches from Jude. She stopped, and again, her gaze steadied on his face. Those pale gray eyes engulfed him, conveying confusion, pain, and behind driving them all, an overwhelming sadness. In her eyes, he saw a bit of himself, and deep down on some level below intellect, they connected.

"Are you the young man collecting money to buy the little boy his bicycle?"

Jude had never heard her speak before and was surprised by her precise elocution. "Yes. I am."

She grabbed his wrist with fingers like steel clamps, turned his palm upward, and pressed coins into it. She spoke with awesome vehemence. "Children are the most important thing in the world."

A strange passion radiated from her, and she trembled as if lightning flowed into her body and found no way to the ground. "You understand. I know you do." She added more softly. "I see it in your eyes."

Her expression reminded Jude of his own mother's ferocity when, for some reason, she'd thought he had been wronged. He looked down and saw in his palm, a quarter, a nickel, and a penny.

It was all Gray Lady had, and he knew it as surely as he could predict the next beat of his heart. He held the coins out to her. "I think you need this more than we do."

"No," she said, shaking her head violently. The woman grabbed his fingers and forced them around the coins. His hand ached with the power of that bony grasp.

"Take the money. It will help . . ." Her eyes looked inward, confused, as if she sought a word to describe something. Then, she smote her breast with her open palm. "It will help me." A plea for understanding vibrated in her voice, in her eyes, and in her trembling body.

The three small coins suddenly felt heavy in his hand. "Thank you." The words came out raspy and choked. "It will help."

The woman shivered with such passion, she seemed about to collapse, but abruptly, she turned on her heel and plodded away. A powerful surge of compassion and empathy for this tragic woman threatened to overcome Jude. Tears dampened his eyes, and he fought to stem them before they betrayed his vulnerability. He averted his gaze and pretended to stare at the sky.

"You don't have to hide from me," said Lonesome. She took his chin, forcing him to look at her, and he saw her dark blue eyes shimmering. Suddenly, they were in each other's arms, and Jude wasn't sure why. But he made no protest and held her until their sadness passed.

Lonesome stepped back and with the tips of her fingers, brushed the moisture from the corner of his eyes. "Now no one will ever guess you bared a little of your soul."

"Are you making fun of me?" Jude tried a grin but knew it was weak.

"No," she said and smiled wisely. "Sometimes, you can be almost inhumanly self-contained. For a split second, I saw through the wall."

Her perceptiveness disconcerted him. It was time to change the subject. Opening his hand, he held the coins out to her. "Would you hang on to these? I have a bad habit of losing change."

She gave him a knowing smile, took the coins, and dropped them into her shirt pocket.

Jude was relieved that a noise interrupted them; a strange flopping sound came from an old sedan approaching from the south. "Flat tire," he said. "That might bring in a few bucks." He waved the car into the turnout.

As it approached, he sighed. He wouldn't be able to charge for this one. An elderly woman sat behind the wheel, obviously close to tears. On the back of the seat next to her sat a big red and gold parrot. The woman rolled down her window. When Jude bent down to speak, the parrot squawked its disapproval and gave him a surly look. The woman's eyes looked teary, and her chin quivered when she spoke. "Something's wrong with my car."

"Just a flat tire," Jude assured her. "If you've got a spare, I'll change it for you."

With a shriek so loud it hurt Jude's ears, the parrot hopped onto the woman's shoulder and snapped its beak at him.

"Shush," said the woman. "This young man's just trying to help." She gave Jude a helpless look. "Fred is very protective."

"Fred?"

"I named him after my late husband." She stroked the bird's back, and he sidled up against her head, sputtering at Jude.

"Why don't you pop the trunk open," Jude said. "I'll see if you have a spare."

"Oh, God bless you, young man." She fumbled under the dash and finally, with a click, the trunk opened.

Lonesome helped him jack up the wheel and take it off. They found a spare and put it on. The sun beat down on his back, and Jude began to feel lightheaded. The queasiness from this morning had never quite left him, and his head ached.

Across the highway, a sixteen-wheeler truck rumbled as it slowed and pulled into the Marina parking lot. A short annoying blast from the air horn sliced into Jude's aching head like a dull axe. A fat, bearded driver crawled down from the cab, looking smug for having announced his presence to the world.

Jude tightened the last lug nut. "I hope Willy's doing better than we are." So far, he and Lonesome had made only two dollars. He couldn't ask the old woman for money, and he knew Lonesome would agree.

As if she'd divined his thoughts, Lonesome spoke. "We only got a couple of hours till noon." She held the hub cap while he pounded it into place. "This isn't a matter of life or death, Jude."

"We don't know that. Anything could be life or death."

She gave him an odd look but did not reply. Jude closed the trunk and with feet dragging, made his way back to the front door. He bent down to speak.

"You're okay now lady," he said. "Just make sure you get that tire fixed soon."

She began to fumble in her purse. Jude held up his hand. "I won't take any money."

Suddenly, the old woman looked past Jude. Her expression turned to horror, her eyes grew wide, and her mouth opened in silent protest. Jude turned his head in time to see Bad Kitty gathering himself to leap. The cat's eyes were fixed on Fred the Parrot.

Bad Kitty sprang onto Jude's back, and using him as a springboard, vaulted into the car. But he misjudged the position of the steering wheel, tripped on it, and missed the parrot.

Fred screeched, a sound that would have done credit to an exploding boiler. He snapped his powerful beak at Bad Kitty, flapped wildly through the window, and escaped, scattering feathers. The woman screamed. Jude jumped back and fell over Lonesome.

Fred made a short, steep glide to the ground and landed shrieking. Bad Kitty came out of the car in a graceful arc that took him over Jude and Lonesome, still struggling to regain their feet. Jude swatted at the cat but missed.

The woman cried out. "His wings are clipped. He can't fly."

Clipped wings notwithstanding, when Bad Kitty pounced, Fred flew. He didn't fly well, but he managed to gain altitude and bank toward the highway.

The woman wailed as Fred cleared the top of a speeding pickup. With vigorous flapping, he climbed again, crossed the highway, and reached the branches of a small tree less than a foot from the parked big rig. The branches, too small to hold his weight, bent slowly, and the big bird hopped casually onto the top of the van.

Jude untangled himself from Lonesome and ran toward the truck, but Bad Kitty was ahead of him running with his eyes fixed on Fred. The tomcat crossed the highway, a heartbeat in front of a speeding truck.

From behind, Lonesome grabbed Jude's arm. "Be careful."

When the traffic cleared, Bad Kitty had climbed the tree and was balanced on the same small limb that had barely supported Fred. Gathering his concentration, the cat jumped, caught the top edge of the van, and scrambled on top.

Jude crossed the highway and ran to the back of the van where a narrow ladder provided access to the top. He clambered up, and as he came over the edge, saw Bad Kitty crouched, tail twitching. Fred faced the cat with his beak open, ready to fight.

As Jude pulled himself onto the top, Bad Kitty pounced.

"Oh my God," screamed the old woman. "He's got my bird."

Jude's assessment of the situation left some room for doubt about who actually had who. There was at least as much cat hair flying as bird feathers. Fred squawked, battered the cat with his wings, and bit clumps of hair and skin from his back.

Bad Kitty squalled and clawed at Fred's chest feathers, but without any lasting harm. Jude ran to them, grabbed Fred in one hand, Bad Kitty in the other, and yanked them apart. Bad Kitty sunk his claws into Jude's hand, and Fred's powerful beak locked into a chunk of flesh at the base of his thumb. Jude added his own howl of pain to the din.

He stumbled back and fell against one of the hot exhaust stacks. When he jerked away, his foot slipped over the edge, and he fell. The fall itself took a long time, and when he struck the soft dirt, the air was driven from his lungs. Dust flew all around him, and swarming spots obscured his vision. Still, Fred gnawed at his thumb, and Bad Kitty clawed at his hand. Jude tossed the tomcat aside and tried to rise, but he couldn't seem to make his legs work.

Then the old woman was over him, gently removing Fred from his grasp. Lonesome appeared and slapped him firmly on the back. Finally, he was able to draw air into his paralyzed lungs.

The screeching sound he made frightened Lonesome.

"Jude, should I call an ambulance?"

He shook his head and screeched again as his lungs filled tortuously. After a few minutes, he could breathe without too much pain, but his hands looked as if he'd jammed them in a shredder.

Lonesome took his hands and tried to wipe away some of the blood with her shirt.

"Are you sure you're all right?"

"I think I've still got most of my major body parts."

She laughed with him, but there were tears in her eyes.

The old woman stood behind Lonesome, stroking Fred and cooing to soothe him. She held the bird close and patted Jude's shoulder.

"Thank you. You saved Fred's life."

"I'm not so sure about that," said Jude. "Fred was more than holding his own."

Lonesome put her arm around him and helped him to his feet. He looked around and saw Bad Kitty sitting near the truck, licking his wounds.

The cat glared at Jude, gave Fred a look of respect, and sauntered away.

Back at the woman's car, she took a ten dollar bill from her purse and pressed it on Jude.

"Fred's my best friend. I can depend on him more than I can my own kids. You take this money, young man."

Momentarily, he weighed his own pride against little Toby's need.

"Thank you, mam," he said. "It will go for a good cause."

She waved to them as she pulled out into traffic. Lonesome took Jude's arm.

"Come on. I'm taking you to the Shack and washing some of your wounds."

Jude didn't object because, in truth, he didn't feel well at all. When they entered the Shack, they found Ed sitting on a stool. He saw Jude, and his jaw dropped.

"Good God, buddy. I didn't look that bad when they hauled me out of the jungle on a stretcher. What the hell happened?"

"It's a long story," said Lonesome. "Vinny bring me some hot water and a towel. Jude can tell you about it while I take care of those cuts."

CHAPTER ELEVEN

When Lonesome finished washing off the blood, Jude's cuts and scratches didn't look so bad, but he felt weary and wrung out.

"You look pretty used up," said Lonesome.

"She's right," said Ed. "Why don't you lay down for a while? Lonesome and I can finish this."

"We started together, we'll finish together." Jude pulled on the clean shirt Lonesome had brought him. "How much did you make?"

Ed reached into his pocket and took out a small wad of bills and some change.

"Six fifty," he said. "Four for scraping the bottom of a boat, a dollar for washing down the gas dock, and I found fifty cents in the pay phone."

"With the twelve Lonesome and I made, we only need ten dollars and fifty cents."

"Maybe Willy had a good day," said Lonesome.

"He called," Vinny informed them. "He and Sherm just snuck out the back door of Barny's a few minutes ago. The crowd was getting rowdy."

"We're not going to make it by noon," Jude said disheartened.

"Maybe we could talk to Toby and explain," Lonesome suggested.

"I was hoping we wouldn't have to do that," said Jude. "But it's better than disappointing him." Tiredly, he climbed off the stool.

"I'll go with you," said Lonesome.

At the door to Shelly's apartment, Jude stopped. "If Toby has had one of his treatments, he may not feel very good."

"I hope we can make him feel a little better," said Lonesome.

Jude knocked on the door, but no one answered.

From across the street, a voice hailed them.

"Can I help you?" It was an old woman standing on the stoop of a small house.

"We were looking for Toby," said Jude.

"I'm his babysitter," said the woman. "They're not back from the hospital yet, but I expect them before four. Shelly has to work at the steak house tonight. Would you like to leave a message?"

"No thanks," said Jude. "We'll come back."

As they made their way to the Shack, Lonesome spoke. "Maybe we've got a few more hours."

"Hope it's enough," said Jude.

Inside the Shack, Vinny set up a round of beers. "This is on the house. You guys deserve it."

They sipped their beer and waited for Willy and Sherm. Ed leaned against a divider column and dozed. Lonesome sat next to Jude, quietly combing the dried salt from her hair. She seldom spoke unless she had something important to say; she was probably the quietest woman he'd ever known. Vaguely puzzled, he wondered why he had never noted that quality before.

A sound came from the alley, and Willy slipped in the back door, an expression of disgust and frustration dragging down his lips.

"How did you do?" asked Jude.

"Only made two dollars," said Willy. "That bunch of college dinks couldn't play worth a shit, but they knew they were being hustled. Wouldn't bet more than a quarter."

Jude sank down on a stool. He felt as if all the bones had been removed from his legs.

"Sorry, Jude. I tried."

"I know you did."

"Sherm made three dollars arm wrestling, but it still ain't enough."

"Three dollars," exclaimed Lonesome.

"Yeah," Willy replied. "It was Sherm's idea. He bet the dinks fifty cents apiece he could beat all six in a row. A couple of them were wrestlers and figured it was a sure thing."

"That gets us a little closer," said Jude. "Where's Sherm now?"

"Over at Vinny's changing clothes."

"Good," said Vinny. "I don't want him sleepin' in my only suit." The phone rang and he answered. "Willy's right here. Want to talk to him?" Vinny gave the handpiece an odd look and hung up. "Bad news, Willy. That was Cragen. He's on his way."

"Shit," said Willy. "Maybe I'll just disappear for a while. I'm too tired for his crap."

"Might be a good time to face him," Jude advised.

"Face him hell," said Ed. "It's time to face the bastard down."

A shudder ran through Willy. "It's not that easy. Uncle Cragen's bad enough, but that bodyguard of his—Yuri." Willy shook his head slowly. "He's worked for my uncle for ten years, and I've never seen him smile."

"If you want, Willy," said Lonesome, "we'll all stay here with you. We won't interfere, but we'll be behind you one hundred percent."

"You don't understand," said Willy. "Yuri carries a gun."

"A gun doesn't make him a tough guy," said Ed.

"Besides," said Jude, "he isn't going to even think about using it with this many witnesses."

Willy combed his hair with his fingers and straightened his shirt.

"Okay, but I don't want anybody getting hurt."

Sherm walked in the front door looking over his shoulder. He stopped and looked puzzled.

"White Mercedes."

A confused look crossed Willy's face. "Cragen doesn't drive a Mercedes."

Outside, a car door slammed, and Jude looked out the front window to see the yuppie standing by the driver's door while Gill climbed reluctantly out the other side.

"It's not Cragen," Jude replied.

"I'll be damned," said Lonesome. "That's the two guys that stiffed us for a dollar."

The yuppie strutted through the door, a phony smile on his face, although it wasn't quite as insolent as this morning. Gill followed behind, trying to be inconspicuous.

The yuppie held out his hand to Jude. "My name is Sterling. The guy at the marina told me

I'd probably find you here." He laughed, a sound that had a feigned sense of camaraderie. "I didn't want you to take my little joke too seriously."

Jude ignored the proffered hand. "Maybe I'm a little confused." He put his fingers to his temple. "But I've always thought jokes were supposed to be funny." He looked around the room. "I don't see anybody laughing."

"Hey," Sterling barked. His eyes lost their feigned humor and turned hard.

"Hey, what?" said Jude. "Are you asking for cattle feed or expressing your displeasure? Because I'm not buying your bullshit."

Sterling's eyes were glass hard now.

"I came here to give you the dollar. Instead, I may just have to kick your ass."

Jude laughed, a hearty sound full of real humor. "You're a phony, smart-mouthed prick." Jude's voice took a hard edge. "Real tough guys don't make threats."

Sterling tried to stare Jude down and failed. Behind him, Gill seemed to shrivel and pulled into himself. Even his expression was neutral. Sterling slipped an eelskin wallet out of his jacket pocket and extracted a dollar bill. "I haven't got time for this shit. Here's your dollar."

"Keep it," said Lonesome. "You're just a petty thief, and we don't need your money."

Sterling turned to look at Lonesome, started to say something, and changed his mind. His look of contempt returned, and with a casual gesture, he tossed the bill at Jude. It struck Jude's chest and fluttered slowly to the floor.

"Pick it up." Jude said the words softly, but they crackled like a splintering iceberg.

Everyone in the room was suddenly quiet and still. No one had ever heard Jude use that tone before.

Sterling took a breath and looked around. No one moved, no one spoke. The sense of cool dislike vanished, and in its place, something darker and more dangerous lurked. Ed's eyes had grown black and unreadable, Willy fingered a pool cue, and Sherm sat as still as an executioner. Even the normally gentle Vinny looked taut and angry.

Comprehension began to change Sterling's expression. Here, his familiar set of rules didn't apply. Words, threats, and trickery were robbed of their power, given no more import than the illusions of a second rate magician. The contempt disappeared from his countenance, replaced in degrees by fear. It came to him slowly that he was an alien here, as much out of his element as a goldfish in a pool of sharks.

Slowly, he bent down and picked up the bill. An expression of intense relief crossed Gill's face. Holding out his hand as if to ward off evil, Sterling placed the money on the bar.

"Look, we're leaving. I don't want any trouble."

"Already got trouble," Ed said softly. "Trick now is to get out of it in one piece."

Sterling's face paled, and Gill became a mere shadow. Slowly, they backed out of the door.

When they were gone, Jude stared after them. Lonesome put her hand on his shoulder.

"Let it go, Jude. They're not worth ten seconds of anger."

Jude grabbed the dollar bill, dipped it in the sink behind the bar, and rolled it between his palms until it formed a soggy, pale green spindle. Vinny grinned, yanked open a drawer under the cash register, and took out an enormous rubber band. He tossed it to Jude. Jude strung it between his thumb and forefinger and loaded it with his wet dollar bill. Stepping to the door, he saw Sterling through the open car window, fumbling to shove a key into the ignition. Pulling the rubber band back to his ear, Jude aimed and released. His marksmanship was unerring, and the bill made a wet splat against the side of Sterling's surgically perfect nose.

Sterling chose to outwardly ignore the final insult; he didn't turn his head or wipe away the damp spot left by the soggy missile. He started the Mercedes and gunned the engine until it screamed. Gravel sprayed higher than the roof as the big sedan fishtailed its way onto the highway. Immediately, the blare of an air-horn rattled the windows, followed by the guttural scream of sliding truck tires. Only at the last instant did the Mercedes come under control enough to miss the truck only by inches.

"Bet Sterling spends the rest of the day cleaning out his pants," said Jude. Behind him, Willy laughed.

Vinny peered out the door. "Must be our day for fancy white cars. There's a limousine pulling in."

Willy's laughter choked off, and he groaned.

From outside came the sound of wide tires popping on gravel, and a big white limousine pulled up and stopped.

"It's Cragen," said Willy. "I hope to hell I'm ready for this."

For a long time, the limousine sat in the sun, its darkened windows reflecting the passing traffic. Then the driver's door opened slowly, and a man got out. A black blazer sporting brass buttons strained to accommodate his barrel chest and gray pinstriped pants failed to conceal legs as thick as those of a bull rhino. Placing a chauffeur's cap carefully on his head, he walked around the car and into the Shack.

Just inside the door, he stopped as his pale gray eyes adjusted to the gloom. He stood utterly still, as if nothing could disturb or move him. Heavy Slavic lips hid beneath a nose so battered it had simply collapsed against his thick cheekbones. Hands like backhoes hung from massive arms. When he spied Willy, no change came over his expression; he merely dismissed the rest of the room.

"Your uncle wishes to speak to you." The words were spoken with a barely detectable accent.

"I'm not really interested in talking to him, Yuri," said Willy. "You can tell him that."

Yuri ignored the remark. "If you will come out to the car." The words sounded more like a threat than a request.

"Tell him to come inside if he wants to see me." Willy's voice quivered, but he kept his expression under control.

Yuri stood monumentally still; a gnarled cypress would have exhibited more movement. After a time, he stepped forward and held out his big hand. "You will come with me, please."

Jude slid off his stool.

Yuri's head snapped around, and his cold gray eyes held Jude's. When Jude refused to drop his gaze, Yuri moved slightly, and his coat folded away from the butt of a holstered automatic.

Jude leaned forward and shook his head slightly. "You've been around long enough to know when a bluff isn't going to work."

Yuri simply stared, his expression as flat as sheet ice, but for just an instant, Jude thought he saw a gleam of humor in Yuri's eyes. Finally, the man shrugged, and the butt of the pistol was again hidden by his jacket. He turned to Willy. "I will relay the message to your uncle."

With a relentless, lumbering stride, Yuri rumbled out of the room. After he entered the limousine, some time passed with no indication of human activity. When Yuri reemerged, he again carefully donned his cap and opened the rear door. A thin, bony man wearing a dark gray suit got out. Although tall, he walked with his head stooped, his eyes peering up from under bushy eyebrows.

Inside, he too paused to let his eyes adjust, but his head turned and twisted, taking stock of the situation. Yuri stepped around the man and stood near the bar.

Cragen's thinning hair was gray and severely combed, his face shiny from a recent shave. His eyes sought out Willy.

"You are very uncooperative today." His voice was the harsh wheeze of a steam pump.

After a sip of beer, Willy looked his uncle over. His face was pale, but he looked determined.

"You really need to get a dictionary, Cragen."

Cragen didn't reply but lifted his eyebrows questioningly.

"The word cooperate doesn't mean do it your way," said Willy. "Now, what did you want to talk about?"

"Perhaps we could find some place more private, William."

"You only call me William when you're trying to irritate me. If you do it again, this conversation is over."

Cragen smiled, a thin lipped baring of teeth that conveyed all the humor of a hungry wolverine.

"My, you are touchy today. But no matter, I simply don't want to discuss family business in the presence of strangers."

"They're only strange to you, Cragen. But I'll make you a deal. You loan me twenty dollars, and I'll go wherever you want."

Slowly, Cragen shook his head. "You know how I feel about such things."

"It's not for me," said Willy. "There is a very sick little boy who wants a bicycle for his birthday. We need just a few dollars more."

"I am genuinely sorry about the little boy, but you know my policy." His cold gray eyes shifted slightly. "However, since you won't discuss this in private . . ." He took a sheaf of papers from his inner jacket pocket.

"If that is the trust fund and power of attorney again," said Willy, "I've already told you to forget it."

"You seem to need money," said Cragen. "And this will provide you with an income for the rest of your life."

"And all I have to do is sign over control of my father's share of the company to you?"

"I control the company now, and it's quite successful. There's no reason for that to change."

"And if I don't sign?"

"If the courts agree with my suit, you will get nothing. I may even gain control of your mother's share."

Cragen gave Willy a smirk so repulsive, it sickened Jude.

"You've just proved you're incompetent to handle money," said Cragen. "The sixty dollars you received yesterday is already gone." The smirk became triumphant.

At first, Willy looked crushed by Cragen's statement. But slowly, a light came to his expression, and a grin spread across his face. He looked his uncle deliberately in the eye.

"How the hell did you know I got sixty dollars yesterday?"

Cragen's eyes flew open, and for just an instant, his expression registered shock. Quickly, he smoothed out his countenance. "Quite simple really—"

"Stuff it," said Willy. He pushed himself away from the bar and stood up, his eyes cold. "You old bastard. You got to my lawyer." Willy thought a moment and laughed. "He used to send me a couple of hundred a month. Now I'm lucky to get sixty." Shaking his head in mock wonder, Willy continued. "How much did it cost you?"

"I have no idea what you are babbling about."

"Another thing," said Willy. "You only accuse people of babbling when they've got your ass pinned to a wall."

Cragen took a step forward still clutching the sheaf of papers. "We digress. If you will sign this—"

"Up your ass, old man," said Willy. "You've heard something. The probate is just about finished, and you think you know what the outcome will be. You've probably got a pipeline to the judge."

"Now be reasonable, nephew."

"Oh I am," said Willy. "For the first time in my life I am being entirely reasonable. Your challenge to my dad's will is failing. This is just a last gasp attempt to buy me off."

Cragen straightened and glared at Willy. "It is no such thing."

Willy's expression steeled, and for an instant, Jude could see the family resemblance.

"You hounded my poor father into his grave and my mother into alcoholism."

"Your father was a weak man."

"Yes, he was," said Willy. "But a kind one. He had the brains, but you had the whip. And when he died, you turned my own mother against me or frightened her into submission. You intended to starve me until I gave in to whatever you wanted. Well, it didn't work. I survived."

Willy gestured, taking in the whole room. "I've got more friends in this room than you've had in your whole life.

"First, I'm going to pick up that poor alcoholic mother of mine, and I'm going to get her help." He stood over Cragen, and the old man seemed to have shrunk. "Then I'll take the forty eight percent of the stock my father left me and the five percent my mother owns, and I'll take over. I'll turn that company into something besides a prison for the people who work there, and then I'm going to kick your useless ass out."

Cragen drew himself up.

"You will try."

With genuine enjoyment, Willy laughed. "You've got a little time, Cragen. But when probate is settled, then you had better get your ass backed up in a corner."

"Your threats are childish," said Cragen, but the words sounded desperate now.

Willy waved his hand dismissively. "Unless you intend to loan me money, take a hike. I've got something important to finish."

Cragen stood staring. Several times, he started to say something but thought better of it. Finally, he turned and wordlessly walked out the door. Willy followed, and as he passed Yuri, the big man put his hand on Willy's shoulder. Sherm stood up glaring, but Willy shook his head at his friend. Yuri whispered in Willy's ear, pressed something into his hand, turned, and accompanied Cragen out to the limousine.

Lonesome ruffled Willy's hair. "Way to go, friend."

"Shit, Willy," said Ed. "Didn't know you had it in you."

"You okay?" asked Jude.

Willy grinned. "My legs are shaking like a wet dog in a snow storm." He held up a hand and in his quivering fingers was a five-dollar bill. "Yuri gave this to me. Said to wish the little boy happy birthday."

CHAPTER TWELVE

Willy's triumphant verbal jousting with Cragen and Yuri's generosity cleared the dark mood of anger and frustration.

Excitedly, everyone piled their contributions on the bar, and Jude swept the money into a pile.

Carefully, he counted it. "Ninety-seven dollars and fifty cents. We need ninety-seven, ninety-nine."

Vinny dug into his pockets and slapped two quarters on the bar. "That's all I got, but now you're a penny over."

"Thirty-two cents over," said Lonesome.

"Right," Jude said softly. "Forgot about Gray Lady's thirty-one cents."

"Gray Lady?" Vinny gave him a strange look. "You talked to Gray Lady?"

Jude told them the story, and everyone sat quietly, enthralled by Gray Lady's mysterious generosity.

"Really strange," said Willy. "Gives me goosebumps. I wonder how she found out about Toby and his bicycle."

"Probably from Pedro, the bus-boy at Old Dan's," said Jude.

Sherm nodded judiciously. "She like Pedro. He try to help her." He stroked his beard. "But maybe she know things because she don't talk — only listen."

It was the longest sentence Jude had ever heard Sherm speak.

"You learn things that way too, Sherm?"

"Sometimes," said the big man.

Ed shook off the mood. "Come on. Let's go buy a bicycle."

"You can take my pickup," said Vinny. "It ain't got much gas, but I think it'll get you to the hardware and back." He gave Jude the keys.

Vinny's pickup lacked any pretense of luxury and was in fact so austere, it lacked some basic necessities. The windshield wipers were mere threads of rotten rubber, but the tires were so slick, driving in the rain would have been suicide anyway. Night driving was almost as hazardous because one headlight pointed to the sky, and the other either blinked with every bump or simply didn't light up at all. Although the engine ran, it was rough and bad tempered with a tendency to stall, usually in the middle of a crowded intersection. The brakes worked but only after vigorous pumping. Vinny believed that if pumping the brakes didn't help, sometimes loud prayers would.

Jude drove with Lonesome seated beside him and Sherm next to the door. Willy and Ed rode in the back. To make room for Sherm's massive shoulders, Lonesome moved closer and placed her arm over the back of the seat. Her breast pressed firmly against Jude's arm. This time, however, his hormones behaved themselves. The desire was there, a banked fire that could easily be fanned into an inferno, but for now she was a comfortable presence, a friend who also happened to be a desirable woman. It was a sensation he had experienced only once in his life. He relished it and at the same time, feared it with his entire being.

The truck's engine bellowed, and the cab rattled and squeaked so loudly, conversation was impossible, but a sense of contentment and satisfaction with their success made discussion unnecessary. They crossed the causeway where, just last night, they had launched their doomed ship. It seemed to Jude that time had been stretched and distorted until he no longer possessed a way of measuring its orderly progress.

The outskirts of Seal Beach came into view, a stolid, quiet little city whose only concession to the wild life was a pair of bars with Irish names and a boisterous Saint Patrick's Day celebration.

The Rite Way Hardware lay outside the center of town. It was a small building with crowded aisles and a confused assortment of hardware littering the shelves. Bins of nails sat next to a wooden keg full of heavy bolts, and above them, hung a rack of denim work aprons. It even smelled of confusion; steel, cloth, leather, and wood all mingled into an aroma that would have been familiar in a turn of the century establishment.

A clerk hurried down the aisle toward them—a short, round fellow with black hair slicked back and a fussy look of concern on his face.

Lonesome chuckled. "He thinks we're here to steal something."

"Can I help you?" asked the clerk.

"A bicycle," said Jude.

The fussy look turned to relief. "Try the bike shop in Belmont Shore. We don't have any adult bicycles."

"That's okay," said Jude. "Because we want one for a little boy."

The clerk looked dubious. "We only have two."

Jude was beginning to lose patience. "That's one more than we need. Why don't you show them to us?"

Nervously, the clerk watched Willy run his fingers along the lacquered wooden handle of a sledgehammer. His gaze shifted abruptly when Sherman picked up a red gas can and peered inside.

Ed let out a long sigh. "Can we get on with this? We haven't got all day."

The clerk glanced around apprehensively but started down the aisle. "They're back here."

He led them to the back where on a shelf, high over the tool rack, sat two small bicycles, one white, and the other blue.

The moment he saw the blue one, Jude knew the cause for little Toby's enthusiasm. Only the frame was painted, the rest was chrome plated or polished aluminum. It was the chain guard that caught his attention. In the chrome plated metal, the silhouette of a rampant pony had been stamped, its mane and tail flowing as if blown by a free wind. Jude knew that at age six, he would have cheerfully murdered strangers to own that bike.

"The blue one."

"They're not exactly alike," said the clerk. "The white one is a deluxe model and —"

"I want the blue one," said Jude savagely.

"Okay." The clerk looked around uneasily. "You want me to get it down for you?"

"I don't intend to buy it to hang on your goddamn wall as a decoration."

"Easy, Jude," said Lonesome.

"I have to get a ladder," said the clerk.

Sherm grabbed a big metal scaffold, lifted it over the counter, and slammed it down under the shelf. "Now, you get bicycle. Okay?"

"Right," said the clerk. Shakily, he climbed on the scaffold and took down the blue bike.

Sherm took it from his hand and examined it, eyes shining. "Good bike."

"Will that be all?" asked the clerk.

Jude began to stack money on the counter. "That's it."

Using one finger, the clerk painstakingly entered the numbers into the old-fashioned cash register, and with a flourish, rang up the sale. He looked up and gave them a reflexive smile.

"That will be one hundred and four dollars and eighty-five cents."

"The price tag says ninety-seven, ninety-nine," said Jude.

He gave them another of his mechanical smiles. "The Governor has to get his share, you know."

Absolute silence greeted his statement. His smile disappeared, and he cleared his throat.

"Sales tax, I have to charge sales tax."

"Son-of-a-bitch." Ed spat out each word like iron shot from a slow fire cannon.

Sales tax. The clerk stood silent, his expression a cold mask of feigned concern, tinged with fear. He didn't seem to be breathing.

Jude felt hollow and weak-kneed, as if he'd stepped in the ring with a heavy-weight boxer. It had been so long since he'd purchased anything of consequence, that sales tax had become a distant, almost forgotten, adversary.

The bloodiest, nastiest last-ditch tax conceived by man, it supposedly struck everyone with the same force. For the rich, it was merely a love tap; to the poor, a brutal knockout punch.

Jude's stomach churned with frustration until he felt as if he was about to throw up.

"Can't you just overlook it this time. This is all the money we've got."

"It's for a sick little boy's birthday," added Lonesome.

"I'm sorry." The clerk shuffled the pile of bills and looked embarrassed. "But I can't. I'd lose my job."

"Can you do anything—personally," asked Willy.

The clerk looked up from the crumpled pile of money.

"I work for minimum wage." The prissy look was gone, and in its place, a quiet desperation. "I literally do not have a dime to my name. Today is payday, but if I piss the old man off, he'll forget to bring my check. If I don't get that check before I go home, I'll have to make excuses to my roommate for not being able to pay the rent."

"Can we talk to the owner?" asked Jude. "He's got to have a heart somewhere."

"Heart." The word dripped sarcasm. "The old bastard's so tight, he doesn't bleed when he's cut." The man's eyes were pleading for understanding now. "You are strong people. You don't give a damn about society and its rules, and I envy you." Resignation dragged at his round face as he pushed the pile of bills back across the counter. "I wish I had that kind of courage, but I don't. I am sorry."

Jude sighed. "Let's get out of here. We've got to find seven dollars somewhere."

The ride back to the Shack was made without any attempt at conversation. Climbing out of the pickup, Jude felt suddenly dizzy and almost fell. He caught himself on the door.

Willy grabbed his arm. "Jude, what the hell's the matter?"

"I'm all right. Just so damn tired."

"Ain't that the truth. We all are."

With a tremendous effort, Jude let go of the door and straightened up.

Lonesome reached up and felt his brow. "Jude, you are burning up with fever."

"Just tired. Let's see if Vinny has got any ideas." He led them into the Shack and felt better in the cool shadows.

Vinny looked up from his chair. "Where's the bike?"

"Forgot about sales tax," said Jude. "We didn't have enough money."

Turning in his chair, Vinny struck a key on the cash register, and the drawer popped open. He collected the money, counted it, and looked up.

"Got just barely enough to pay the beer truck driver." He held up two one dollar bills. "You can have what's left over."

"We'll keep it in mind," said Jude. "But hang on to it for now." He slumped over the bar. "Does anyone have an idea?" His gaze traveled from one face to another. He saw nothing but grim exhaustion, desperation, and even more disturbing, the first traces of defeat.

CHAPTER THIRTEEN

Blowing in through a half open window, a hot, dry breeze stirred cobwebs hanging from the ceiling. A shaft of light crossed the room, and dust motes rushed through it in a swirling, single-minded stream. Jude watched them and wondered if they possessed a purpose and resolution that kept them constantly in motion. He envied their energy; his own vitality was eroding in the face of relentless frustration.

Across from him, Sherm had his head on the bar, watching drops of water crawl down the side of his glass. Ed slumped against a support post, eyes red and bleary. Willy looked so tired and drawn, he appeared to have shrunk down to almost nothing. Lonesome stood next to Jude, bent over the bar, staring vacantly through the window.

He fought the growing lethargy and tried to find words that would reach his friends, words that would renew their endurance. There was nothing left to say. Words had lost their power, and all that remained was his own obstinate refusal to accept defeat.

A gust of wind blew the door open, and as Jude moved to close it, he saw a figure approaching—an old man leaning on a heavy cane. The man progressed with a swing of the walking stick, followed by a series of quick double steps.

A round head completely devoid of hair and huge, thin ears gave him the air of a genial gargoyle. He grabbed the frame to steady himself as he stepped through the door.

Vinny roused himself from his chair and leaned on the bar. "Johnny Two Step. How are you doing?"

"Not bad considering that I'm older than everybody else in the world put together." Impatiently, he swiped dust from his shoulders. "There's a Santa Ana wind building up."

"That's all we need." Ed's voice echoed the weariness and dejection of the others. "A devil wind."

Johnny took in the small group sitting tiredly around the bar. "Thought I'd find you kids here." He singled out Jude. "Damn, boy, I've seen roadkill in better condition. What the hell happened?"

"Been a bad day, Johnny."

The old man's face clouded with anger.

"So I heard. Just came from Hal's Bait Shop. The old bastard was bragging about screwing you guys out of ten cents a pound for the mackerel." He slammed his cane against the floor in frustration. "When I found out what you was trying to do, I gave him blue, flamin' hell. Told him I'd never buy another damned thing in his store again. Should have whacked him upside the head."

"He's not worth it, Johnny," said Jude.

"Goddamn right he's not. Not worth the powder and shot it would take to blow his narrow ass off. But whackin' him would have sure made me feel better."

Again, he looked the small group over. "You kids look plumb tuckered out." Johnny shook his head slowly. "Guess I don't have to ask if you got enough money. I can see it in your faces."

"We was hoping to get the bicycle before Toby got home from the hospital," said Jude. "But now, I'm not sure we can do it at all."

Johnny gave him an earnest look. "I'd help if I had any money, but I don't."

"I know you would."

"Damn shame," said Johnny. "What you kids are doing is noble, just ain't any other word for it. Nobody's going to thank you, except Shelly and little Toby. Nobody else is even going to notice."

He pointed his cane in the general direction of Surfside. "There's some rich assholes up there going to spend more money today on martinis than it would take to buy that little fellow a bike."

He turned to Vinny. "Is my credit still good in here?"

"You know it is, Johnny."

"Give these kids all the beer they want, and give them some of those pickled eggs. It ain't much, but it's all I can do. I'll pay you when my Social Security check comes in."

"We can't let you do that," said Lonesome.

"Yes you can, pretty girl." He stepped up close, and his eyes held Lonesome's. "You see, there just ain't many really good people left in this old world. This quest of yours has gotten to be kind of a crusade. Not a big one mind you, but important. I want to be a little part of it." He patted her arm. "You'll be doing more for me than the other way round."

Lonesome smiled. "Thank you, Johnny."

When the beer was poured, Johnny raised his glass in a toast. "Long life and good friends."

They all drank together, and Vinny passed out the pickled eggs. Jude sipped his beer slowly but found he couldn't eat.

"Better eat something," said Lonesome.

"Maybe later, when my stomach settles."

Lonesome started to speak but instead shook her head and said nothing.

Johnny finished his beer and using his cane, hauled himself to his feet. "Got to go. The Senior Citizens Center in Seal Beach is having a free lunch for us old codgers." He stopped and thought. "I got an idea. I could probably do a little fast talking and get some food for you kids."

"Couldn't let you do that," said Jude. "We'd be taking food from someone that really needs it."

Johnny studied Jude's face. "I might've known you'd say something like that." Again, he stumped his cane on the floor. "By God, I always figured you kids had class. Now I know it for sure."

He made his way to the door, looked toward the bay, and laughed. "You want to see something funny." He motioned for them to join him. "Some rich kid has run his boat ashore on the mud flat."

Across the highway and somewhat north, where the causeway crossed the channel, Anaheim Bay became a huge sheet of mud at low tide and a shallow marsh at high. About a hundred yards from shore and less from the causeway, a small cruiser sat with its bow riding up into the mud. The turning tide would soon leave it completely stranded. A young man climbed off the boat and sloshed his way across the mud, flat toward the highway.

Johnny hobbled down the steps. "Not really funny, I guess. Just some dumbass with more money than brains." He waved to them as he walked away.

Behind him, Jude heard Sherman mutter. "More money than brains. Maybe he got seven dollars."

The room grew quiet, but now with anticipation. Willy stood up and finished his beer, life returned to Ed's eyes, and Lonesome joined Jude at the door.

"What are you thinking, Sherm?" asked Jude.

Sherm screwed up his face and stroked his beard. "Think I go talk to guy with stuck boat."

"I'm with you," said Jude. An inspiration from Sherman was a rare event and not much hope, but at the moment, it was all he had.

As they made their way across the highway, Lonesome caught up. "Sherm, do you have an idea?"

"Maybe."

When they reached the far side, a young man was climbing up the side of the highway embankment.

About seventeen or possibly older. He was thin and dark haired with a strip of skin across his shoulders burned bright red. He turned and looked at the boat. "Oh man! My dad's going to kill me."

Sherm stopped and surveyed the mud flat. "Need help?"

"Shit yeah, I need help. Need a miracle. I ain't got the money for a tow boat, so I've got to call my dad." The boy scraped mud from his legs. "He'll give me a lecture and ground me, and I'm supposed to take Karen to the concert tonight." He was almost in tears.

"You got ten dollars?" asked Sherm.

The boy looked up, his mouth hanging open, and a spark of hope lighting his eyes. "Don't think I've got ten, but if you'd trust me . . ."

"How much you got?"

The boy extracted his wallet and dug out a thin sheaf of bills. He held it up for Sherm to see.

"Only got five, but I swear if you can get dad's boat out of that mud, I'll get the rest."

Jude put his hand on Sherm's shoulder and spoke softly. "It's almost enough. Take whatever you can get."

Sherm nodded to the boy. "Okay."

The boy's face brightened. "You'll do it?"

"What your name?" Sherm asked.

"Buddy," he grabbed Sherm's big paw and pumped it. "Man, I don't know how to thank you."

Sherm turned to Lonesome. "Where you put shovel?"

"In Vinny's storage shed. Want me to go get it?"

"Okay."

Lonesome started back for the shovel, and the rest stared at the stranded boat.

"Looks impossible to me," said Willy.

"Without a boat," Ed shook his head, "just don't see any way it can be done."

Jude studied the predicament but saw no way to resolve it. "I hope your idea is a good one, Sherm."

He got a solemn look from Sherman. "Me too." He started down the bank into the mud.

The rest followed with Willy hanging back next to Jude. "This doesn't look good, Jude, and we don't have much time."

"I know. I've got my fingers crossed."

"You're going to need a lot of fingers to pull up enough luck to save this one."

The wind whipped and sawed across the flats, as they slogged through the soft, shin-deep mud. When they reached the boat, Sherm walked slowly around the small cruiser and studied it carefully.

It sat more than halfway up on the mud with the stern in the canal. Sherm reached into the deeper water and ran his hand around the rudder and prop.

Jude kneeled down near a through-hull fitting below the water line.

"Looks like you may have a crack in the hull."

The boy leaned down to see. "Shit, there sure is. If it's not too bad, maybe the bilge pump will keep up until I get it to the marina."

On the causeway, a small crowd of spectators had gathered, and a pair of skinny boys hooted derisively. Buddy gave them an embarrassed look. "Couple of guys I go to school with."

Sherm returned from his inspection of the stern. "Prop okay?"

"Yeah," said Buddy. "I tried backing off with the engine, but it's jammed too tight."

"I don't think there's time to shovel it out," Ed said.

"Nope," said Sherm. "No time." Pulling at his beard, he furrowed his brow in concentration. For a while, he stood with his back to the boat and studied the mud flat.

The retreating tide was draining from the higher ground back into the main canal, most of it through a shallow channel about thirty feet from the boat. Soon, the entire mud flat would be above the water line, and the boat stranded until next high tide.

"I've watched these tides," said Willy. "We got about an hour, maybe a little more."

Buddy looked disappointed, and his thin shoulders drooped dispiritedly.

"I guess I better go call my dad."

"No," said Sherm. "We do it." He looked over his shoulder. "Here come Lonesome with shovel."

Lonesome was crossing the mud, her long legs dripping black goo. Behind her, Jude could see under the causeway and into the outer harbor where a flotilla of small yachts were making their way toward the inner harbor.

"Looks like the boaters have found out about the Santa Ana."

"Smart," said Willy. "A savvy skipper gets his ass ashore when a devil wind blows."

Lonesome arrived and stuck the shovel in the mud. She gave Sherm a tired grin.

"Okay, boss. What do we do now?"

Sherm looked embarrassed. "I show how, but you help me with big words?"

"Of course I will, Sherm."

"You're the boss, Sherm," said Ed. "And Lonesome's your foreman."

"Need lots of sticks," said Sherman. He held his hands open shoulder width.

"What do we use them for?" asked Jude.

"Pound them in dirt." He pointed to the runoff channel. "All across." "Then . . ." He waved his arm back and fourth, parallel to the ground.

"He wants more sticks laying across the uprights," said Lonesome.

Sherm nodded emphatically. "Sticks, paper, grass, anything."

"What the hell for?" asked Willy.

"A dam," Jude explained. "Sherm wants us to build a dam just like beavers do."

A big grin lit Sherm's face. "Yes. We be fisherman, we be mules, now we be beavers."

"Then what?" asked Willy. He looked dubious.

"Dig . . ." Sherm pointed to the ground and looked to Lonesome for help.

"A ditch?"

"Yes. Ditch to boat. Water go to boat and wash away mud."

"Damn," said Jude. "Divert the runoff to the boat. It just might work."

Sherm beamed. "Work fast," he said.

While Lonesome and Willy scavenged for stakes, Jude and Ed pounded them into the mud across the runoff channel, using rocks as hammers. Sherm used the time to dig a trench from the edge of the channel to the boat where it split and ran along each side of the hull.

Ed helped Jude set the last stake and stood watching Sherm. "I underestimated that big son of a bitch," he said.

"So did I," said Jude. "But maybe we all underrated ourselves."

Everyone pitched in to gather the materials to fill in their dam. Before long, water began to rise, and Sherm opened a way into his ditch. The water ran through around the boat and began to cut away at the mud.

"It's working," said Willy.

The tide, however, was receding rapidly, and the mud wasn't being swept away as fast as the water level fell.

"Come on," said Jude. "Use the shovel and sticks or anything you can find to help loosen the mud."

For an exhausting hour, they worked frantically, scraping and digging mud while Sherm's trench continued to carry away the debris. Suddenly, the boat shuddered and slid a few inches into the water.

"Hop aboard," Jude said to Buddy. "It's about to go."

The boy gave Sherm his money. "You earned it whether the boat goes or not."

He jumped into the boat and started the engine.

Behind him, Jude heard the pulsating whine of a marine engine being driven fast through choppy water. He glanced over his shoulder and saw a low slung power boat, a red ocean racer, coming in from the outer bay.

"That guy is going way too fast," said Lonesome.

"The harbor patrol will stop him," said Jude. Closer at hand, a small sailboat tacked and made its way under the causeway. The man at the helm waved.

Sherm pushed on the bow of the cruiser, and it trembled but moved no farther.

"Let's try rocking it," said Jude.

"Yes," Sherm agreed. "You and Ed this side, me and Willy that side. Lonesome push on the bow." He pointed to Buddy. "You put in reverse. Boat move, you gun engine."

The sailboat, a sloop of about twenty feet and now just yards away, slowed as the man at the helm luffed the sails. The woman seated next to him stood up, cupped her hands, and yelled.

"Need any help?"

"No thanks," said Jude. "We've got it."

He waved them off. The boat came about and tacked toward the far side of the channel. The scream of the racer's engine was closer now, but Jude ignored it.

They began to rock the cruiser gently, and Lonesome pushed on the bow. The boat shuddered, and the mud made a horrible sucking sound as it reluctantly released its grip. Jude joined Lonesome at the bow, and their combined strength was enough. The cruiser began to slide.

The tooth rattling scream of the racer was upon them, and Jude looked up to see the boat angling under the causeway, its rooster tail nearly reaching the bottom of the causeway above. A young man stood at the wheel, his head thrown back, hair streaming. The girl sitting next to him looked suitably impressed.

"Here we go," Buddy yelled. The engine roared, and the boat slipped slowly into the channel.

Impatiently, the young man in the racer spun the helm to port to avoid the cruiser, and in the same instant the sloop, now on the far side of the channel, came about.

Although there remained sufficient room in the channel for safe passage, the young man overreacted and yanked the racer's helm savagely back to starboard, bringing him directly into the wind and the chop it had created.

The speeding boat slammed into the chop and bounced high; the bow rising to a dangerous angle. A gust of wind thrust under the flat keel, lifting the entire boat clear of the water. Airborne, the boat capsized backwards and rolled toward the sailboat.

Jude could see horrified looks on the faces of the couple in the little sloop. The man yanked the tiller over hard, but it was merely a reflex. Nothing could save them.

Stern first, the racer plunged down, crashing into the bow of the sloop. On impact, a gush of water exploded upwards, obscuring everything.

For a heartbeat, no one moved. Buddy pulled the cruiser forward trying to keep it from turning in the heavy wind. He called to those on shore.

"I'm taking on water—fast. I'll try to make it to the marina and call the harbor patrol."

"Call an ambulance too," said Jude.

The air cleared, and brackish water fell like dirty rain. In the water lay a jumble of wreckage. The racer floated upside down, tangled in a mess of sails and rigging still attached to the sailboat. Only the stern of the sailboat remained afloat, and Jude could see bubbles boiling the surface.

"Life jackets," said Willy pointing. The couple in the sailboat had been wearing life preservers, and now Jude could see the bright orange vests. They were both trying to swim, but the man moved feebly and without coordination. The woman reached for him, but the current carried him just beyond her grasp.

Willy and Sherm were on the water's edge, and without hesitation, dived in. Both were strong swimmers and took only seconds to reach the couple already being swept by the current into the channel toward the outer bay. Jude heard the rumble of a powerful diesel engine and saw a navy patrol boat crossing the bay toward them.

He started toward the channel, thick mud sucking at his feet. No sign of the pair in the racer. Lonesome's harsh breath came from behind him as she struggled to keep up.

"They may be trapped inside," he said.

The wreckage had drifted a few feet and snagged on a navigation buoy. Somewhere inside the racer's hull, a big bubble of air was trapped. With luck, the two people might be in it.

"I'm going out there," Jude said and dove in.

The current was strong, and he was forced to swim at an angle to keep from being swept past the racer. He grabbed at the bright red hull, but it was glass smooth and provided nothing to use as a handhold. Swimming against the current, he rounded the half-submerged hull, and his grasping fingers found a cleat on the buoy. He paused, breathing deeply, saturating his lungs with oxygen. Rolling forward, he dived like a seal and swam down, his hand groping blindly for the gunwale.

No opening; he was too far forward. Sliding his hand down, he felt something sharp and jagged. The broken windscreen. He dived deeper, almost out of air. Estimating the position of the cabin opening, he swam up. His head broke the surface inside the broken hull. He gasped in air that smelled of gasoline. It was dark, but just enough light refracted by the water entered for him to see the face of a girl in front of him.

"Are you all right?"

She didn't answer. Her eyes looked unfocused, and her head moved unsteadily. She held the broken steering wheel in one hand, and in the other, what looked like a fistful of hair.

Jude reached down, and his groping fingers found a head. Reaching deeper, he grabbed a fist-full of cloth and lifted. The pale bleeding face of the driver surfaced, but with the boy's nose and mouth barely clear of the surface, Jude found he could lift no farther. Somewhere below, out of sight, the boy's body was caught. Jude leaned close and heard a soft breath, then a weak cough.

Jude turned to the girl, but she was slipping down into the water, her expression slack. He grabbed her hair and pulled her head up, kicking vigorously to keep them both afloat. Water slapped him in the face, and he coughed violently; he didn't have the breath to scream for help.

Water erupted in front of him, and a face appeared. Lonesome.

"The girl," he managed to croak.

Lonesome understood immediately and took the girl, holding her above the water.

"Jude, the sailboat's sinking," said Lonesome. "It's going to drag this whole damn thing down with it."

"Can't leave," he gasped. "The boy is stuck. Get the girl out of here and send help."

She gave him a desperate look, and a sound came from her throat that was neither a word nor a cry. With one hand, she pinched the girl's nose shut and covered her mouth.

"She may fight you," said Jude.

"I know. I'll be back." She ducked beneath the surface, carrying the girl with her.

The current pulling against his body strengthened, and keeping the boy's face above the water became increasingly difficult. The boat jerked and vibrated, and a grinding sound came from outside. Something bumped his leg, and Willy surfaced, gasping.

"You got to get outta here, Jude. This junk is about to come loose from the buoy."

"I can't leave this guy to drown. Dive down, and see if you can tell what's holding him."

"Okay, hang on." Willy sank from sight, and Jude could feel the man moving near his feet. Willy surfaced, and wiped water from his eyes. "It's a piece of rope wound round his ankle. I couldn't get it loose."

The boat was vibrating badly and weaving in the current.

"Go outside," said Jude. "See if you can stabilize this junk."

Again, Willy sank from sight. The noise and motion grew worse; the edge of the cabin banged painfully against his shoulder. The constant effort of treading water exhausted him, but he could find nothing on which to brace his feet. Worse, the boy was being pulled down in tiny but inevitable degrees.

The motion and noise began to slacken, and the boat stopped beating at his shoulder.

Willy's face broke the surface.

"Sherm and Ed are on the buoy holding it, but they're not going to be able to last very long."

"What the hell is Ed doing in the water? He can't swim."

"We couldn't stop him. He found one of the sailboat's life vests and jumped in." Willy coughed and spat water. "It's a good thing. I don't think even Sherm could hold this mess alone."

"You find anything to cut the rope with?"

"No time to look," said Willy. "How about your knife?"

"Damnit," said Jude. "I left it in my room." He gulped, swallowed water, and gagged.

"Just below me, there's a broken windscreen. See if you can cut the rope on that."

Willy slipped out of sight, and Jude could feel new tension on the boy's body. A moment later, he reappeared. "Can't quite make it. The rope's too tight."

"Only one thing we can do," said Jude. "I'll take him under to give you some slack." He put his hand over the boy's mouth and nose. "You ready?"

Willy nodded. Jude took a deep breath, and they sank together.

The cold darkness closed around him, and he could feel the boy's body jerk and twist as Willy tried to cut the rope. The pressure in his chest began to build; it become pain, then a burning agony. With a hard wrench on the boy's body, they were free. Desperately, he kicked for the surface, but with a terrible grating sound he could hear even under water, the boat twisted and moved. Something struck him in the back, driving air from his lungs.

For an instant, he floated clear, confused and disoriented, his lungs bursting. Hope fled. Even cold, death-dealing water would be preferable to the torment in his lungs. The slack body in his arms didn't move. Was he about to die trying to save a dead man?

Something touched him, grabbed his hair, and yanked him toward the surface. He broke out of the water, air screamed into his lungs, and again, he sank. And again, the persistent hand jerked him back to the surface. But new hands seized him now, and both he and his limp burden were snatched bodily up onto a rough surface.

For a while, he simply lay still; eyes closed — coughing water — breathing. His head lay on something soft, and he could hear someone crying.

"Jude! Jude!"

Opening his eyes, he realized he lay on the deck of a boat. He turned his head and found it was in Lonesome's lap, and he saw water running down her cheeks. Or was it tears?

In front of him, a man's face appeared, black and shiny as coal, dark brown eyes concerned. There was a sailor's hat perched on his head.

"You all right?" His voice was the deep, gentle rumble of a contented lion.

"Unless I'm dead, and you're an angel."

White teeth flashed in a wide grin. "All the angels I ever seen was white. So, I guess I ain't one." He took Jude's hand and helped him sit up. "Chief Petty Officer Davis." He flashed his spectacular grin. "You can call me Davis."

Struggling, Jude managed to stand up. The boat was a small navy tender used for patrolling the harbor. Ed and Willy sat on a stern bench, and Sherm leaned on the gunwale. One sailor was stationed at the helm, and another stood holding a shore line tied to a piling while attendants loaded the boy into a waiting ambulance.

"Go slow," said Lonesome. "You were under a long time."

"You might not have come up at all, wasn't for this girl," said Davis. "She hauled you up to the top, and me and this big ape here pulled you and that kid onto the boat."

Jude turned to thank Lonesome, but she was looking away to where the ambulance had started up the service road, siren wailing. He started to touch her shoulder, but something in his pants pocket stabbed him painfully. He drew out his harmonica, crushed and broken beyond repair.

"Oh no," said Lonesome.

The rest gathered around as if to view the remains of an old friend.

"Bound to happen some day," Jude said gruffly. But for some reason, he felt saddened as if it were a premonition. He tossed it into the channel. "Burial at sea. It deserves an end like that."

From up on the causeway, a voice shouted. "The news vans are coming."

Davis' chuckle sounded like distant thunder. "There was a camera crew from one of the television stations on the other side of the bay. They filmed what happened. You can bet it will be on the six o'clock news."

"Let's get the hell out of here," Ed insisted.

"Hang on," said Davis. "You guys look about beat to death. Is there anything else we can do for you?"

Jude looked at the others. "There might be. You see, we're trying to collect money to buy a bicycle for a little boy's birthday, and we're a few dollars short."

Slowly, Davis shook his head. "You got to be shittin' me. You risked your lives to pull a couple of kids out of a sinking boat, you look half-starved and dead tired, but all you want is a few bucks to buy a bicycle?"

"That's all," said Willy.

Davis laughed as if he didn't believe what he was hearing. "You're going to be famous."

"Famous won't buy that bicycle," said Lonesome.

For a long time, Davis stared at them. Then he reached in his pocket. "I'm a sailor and sailors never have any money." He held a handful of change. "But by God, you are welcome to what I've got." Turning to the sailor at the helm, he spoke again. "How about you, Seaman Stewart?"

The sailor at the helm, a thin young man with a prominent Adams apple, adjusted the throttle and reached into his pocket. "I only got three and some change, but if it will help." He gave the money to Davis who turned to the sailor holding the shore line.

"You got any money, Bedford?"

"I got a few bucks," said the young sailor. "But I'm outta cigarettes. What are you going to do if I have a nicotine fit?"

"Throw cold water on you."

The boy grinned and passed Davis the money. "Guess I just gave up smoking."

Davis gave Jude the collection of change and bills.

Jude took it, and his hands trembled so badly he almost dropped it. "There is more here than we need," said Jude. "If you give me a minute—"

"Keep it," said Davis. "And don't worry bout us. We get paid Monday, and sailors are used to being broke."

"Thanks," said Jude. "Now a brave little boy will get his birthday present."

With wobbly legs, he walked to the gunwale and started to step ashore. Abruptly, the world spun crazily, and he almost fell. A strong hand grabbed his shirt and steadied him.

"Let me give you a hand." Davis took his arm. "You don't look too good."

"I'm okay. It's just that, in the last twenty-four hours, I must have swallowed half the goddamn ocean." He allowed Davis to help him ashore, and his friends followed.

Davis chuckled delightedly. "You guys really are not going to wait for the reporters, are you?"

"Can't," said Sherm. "Got no time."

When they were all ashore, Davis pushed the boat away from the bank.

"Guess I can tell the guys back at the base that today, I met some real heroes."

"We just hauled a couple of kids ashore," said Lonesome. "Anybody would have done that."

"That wasn't what I was referring to," said Davis. He gave them a snappy salute, and the boat pulled away.

Ed started laughing. "Christ, we don't look like heroes. We look like a bunch of tramps that have been sleeping under the bridge."

Jude joined in, but laughing hurt his chest. He stopped and took a deep breath and felt a nasty rattle down deep inside.

"Let's get Toby's bicycle before the hardware store closes."

CHAPTER FOURTEEN

The second trip to the hardware store seemed shorter than the first, even though they were forced by a sputtering engine to put a dollar's worth of gasoline in Vinny's truck. They crowded through the front door of the Rite Way Hardware and made their way to the back.

The clerk from the morning was gone, replaced by an old man with the neutral expression of a blackjack dealer.

Lonesome stopped, and with a horrified look, pointed to the shelf above the counter. The little blue bicycle was gone.

"What happened to the blue one?" asked Jude.

The old man looked puzzled. "The blue what?"

"Bicycle," said Jude. "It was here this morning."

"Sold it," said the man. "Couple of hours ago. I got a white one though."

"It has to be blue," said Jude.

"Only got the white one. If that won't do, can't help you."

Jude stood stunned and defeated. His eyes felt swollen, and his chest hurt. "Guess we got no choice." He placed the money in a pile on the counter.

The old man rang it up and counted the money. "You're short ten dollars and change."

"That's one hundred and four dollars and eighty-four cents."

"Right," said the old man. "But the bike is one hundred and fifteen dollars and fifty-five cents, including sales tax."

"When did the price go up?" Jude's voice had a dangerous edge the old man recognized.

"The white one is a deluxe model," he said. "It's got three speeds. The blue one was a single speed."

Jude dug in his pocket and took out the handful of money and change collected from the sailors. Carefully, he counted it.

"We're thirty-one cents short," he said dully. Even as he said the words, a mystical sense came over him; a feeling that somewhere, an enchanted gate had opened.

Lonesome looked at him, her eyes wide with disbelief.

Destiny, Karma, fate were all concepts that might be used to explain a peculiar set of circumstances, but they were not philosophical abstractions that fit with Jude's own utilitarian world view. The hair on his arms stood up, a chill shook his body, and for a heartbeat, he marveled at the beauty and symmetry of the Gray Lady's gift.

"Thirty-one cents," he said.

Lonesome reached into her shirt pocket and placed thirty-one cents on the counter.

"Jeez," Ed croaked. "The Gray Lady's money."

"Kinda scary," said Willy. "But it's good mojo."

"Maybe Gray Lady know things we don't," said Sherm.

The magic ended when the old man moved impatiently.

"Do you guys want the bicycle or not?"

"You got any blue paint?" asked Willy.

"Spray cans are on aisle three," said the man. "Dollar fifty a can."

"We only got enough money for the bicycle," said Willy. "How about throwing the paint in free?"

The old man gave him a hard look. "You go out and look at my sign. It says Hardware, but nothing about Charity. You want paint, you buy it."

Jude knew how important a detail like color could be to a small child, but the white bicycle was available, and somehow, he couldn't bring himself to deny an omen as powerful as the Gray Lady's thirty-one cents.

"Maybe we'll think of something later," he said. "We'll take the white one."

Slowly, he counted out the money; exactly one hundred and fifteen dollars and fifty-five cents.

The old man took it and just as carefully, recounted. While he rung up the purchase, Ed began to paw through a pile of metal garbage cans. They slipped from his grasp and crashed to the floor with a terrible racket.

The old man came from behind the counter and gave Ed a hard look.

"You intend to buy a garbage can?"

"Nope."

Impatiently, the old man grabbed the cans and restacked them. With a final glare at Ed, he returned to his task and gave Jude a receipt.

"All sales are final," he said. "Don't bring it back crying about it being the wrong color."

Jude took the receipt and noticed a printed message at the bottom. God bless you and next to the message, a shining light.

"You a religious man?" asked Jude.

A smug, pious look settled on the old man's face. "That's right. Go to church every Sunday. But don't get the idea I'm going to give anything away."

Shaking his head, Jude said, "I learned a long time ago that a man is what he does—not what he says."

They left the old man staring after them. Ed and Sherm took charge of the bicycle in the back of the pickup. Willy climbed into the front seat and sat next to Lonesome.

"Willy, what is the matter with you?" said Jude. "You're prancing around like you got hemorrhoids."

Willy grinned triumphantly, reached into his pants, and pulled out a can of blue spray paint. Another excursion into his baggy pants produced a roll of masking tape.

Lonesome giggled. "So that's why Ed suddenly got so clumsy."

In spite of his churning stomach and burning eyes, Jude felt elated. Finally, they had succeeded.

After returning Vinny's pickup, they took the bicycle to the Shack.

Vinny looked it over and said. "Nice little bike. Any of you guys know how to paint?"

A profound silence settled over them. Sherm shook his head slowly, and Ed said softly. "Hell, I can't paint graffiti."

"I've never painted anything," said Lonesome. Finally Willy spoke.

"I did some model airplanes when I was a kid, but I ain't up to something this important." He gave Jude an earnest look. "I just figured you could do it. You always seem to be able to do anything."

"Can't paint," said Jude. "My hands are shaking too bad."

"My God," gasped Lonesome. "Look at them." She took his hands in hers and looked into his eyes. "Jude, you're sick, really sick. You go lay down, and we'll finish this."

Ed put his hand on Jude's shoulder. "You want us to take you to a doctor. I know where there's a free clinic—"

"No," said Jude. "We need to find a clean place to paint the bike."

"God, you're a stubborn man," said Lonesome. She looked around. "How about the old patio slab by the burned-out house."

"It's close to the highway," said Willy. "But it's protected from the wind. I can't think of anywhere better."

Vinny reached under the bar and brought out a stack of newspapers. "Use these to set it on."

They carried the bicycle to the remains of a house near the highway. A few years previously, it had been a rental, and fire had gutted the interior. The owner never rebuilt or even cleaned up the lot. The patio slab was used regularly for dancing and parties, but it was otherwise abandoned. After spreading out the newspapers, Willy carefully taped everything on the bike that was not to be painted.

Gently, Sherm turned the bike upside down on the papers. With a somber expression, Willy began to shake the paint can.

"How long do you have to shake it?" asked Lonesome.

"One minute after the ball bearing inside starts to rattle."

"Don't hear nothin'," said Sherm.

Ed leaned closer. "I think I can hear it."

Willy decided that if one minute was good, two was better. When the mixing was done, he again carefully read the instructions. Pointing the spray can at a spot on the inside of the fork, he hesitantly pressed the head. With a hiss, a mist of blue paint struck the white and formed a tiny contrasting circle. He stopped and studied the results.

"Maybe you held it too close," said Ed. "Looks like it might be running a little."

"Maybe shake can some more," said Sherm.

"I think it's okay," said Lonesome. "But we got to finish before the sun goes down, or it won't dry."

Behind them, the sound of tires crunching on gravel drew near. Jude looked over his shoulder. A black and white police cruiser stopped at the curb, and the radio sputtered curtly. Deliberately, an officer opened the door, retrieved a baton from the seat next to him, and slid it into a loop on his belt. Not tall, but broad of chest and sturdy of limb, he embodied the ideal uniformed policemen.

Without haste, he walked around the back of his cruiser and started toward them. As he approached, his eyes took in the bicycle and the paint can poised in Willy's hand. He stopped a few feet away.

"Hi guys. Doing some painting?"

"It's a birthday present," said Jude. "The little guy we bought it for wants a blue bicycle, but all we could find was a white one."

The patrolman nodded. "None of you really look like you've got enough money to buy a good bike like this."

"It's a long story," said Jude. "But we raised the money, more or less honestly."

"You got a receipt for it?"

Jude fished the slip of paper out of his pocket.

The officer read it thoughtfully and handed it back. "Okay. Now can I see one for the paint."

Willy sighed nervously. "Don't have one."

The officer took a notepad from his shirt pocket and consulted it. "I just took a report of a stolen can of paint."

"Officer," said Jude. "Will it change anything if we finish painting the bicycle?"

"No. It won't."

"You got time for a story? I'll try to keep it short."

"I'll listen," said the officer.

Jude told an edited version, leaving out those things best not recounted to an officer sworn to uphold the law.

When he finished, Jude added, "The little boy is sick, very sick, and his mother doesn't have money to buy him a birthday present."

"That is the one hell of a story," said the officer. "I wish I could believe it."

"Look," said Jude. "The little boy's mother saved her tips for six months —"

"Tips," said the officer. "Is she a waitress?"

"Yes. She works days at the coffee shop and nights at the steak house."

The officer studied Jude's face. "What's her name?"

"Shelly. I don't know her last name."

"I know Shelly," said the officer. "I eat lunch at the coffee shop every day. She's told me a lot about her little boy."

"If you'll just let us finish the bike, we'll make this whole thing easy for you," said Jude.

The officer studied his notebook for what seemed like a long time. Finally, he returned it to his pocket and spoke to Willy. "Give me the paint."

Slowly, Willy handed it to him. Carefully, the officer studied the can and the blue spot on the bike. "The report I took says the stolen paint was medium blue. This looks light blue to me."

"Definitely light blue," said Willy.

"Very light blue," continued Sherm.

"Don't think I've ever seen a lighter blue," added Ed.

The officer squatted down and scrutinized the little blue circle of paint. "Looks like you're not the world's greatest painter."

"Never painted anything in my life except a model airplane."

The officer nodded and expertly began to paint the bicycle.

Between strokes, he said. "Did this a lot in high school. I'd buy old bikes, fix them up, and sell them. That's how I bought my first car." He stepped back. The little bicycle was now a soft ocean blue. He tossed the can to Willy. "Make sure you dispose of this light blue paint can in a proper manner."

"Right," said Willy.

The officer hitched up his heavy belt and looked up and down the street.

"Is there a bakery around here?"

"In the market," said Jude.

"You guys wait here," said the officer. "You've got to let that paint dry for a while anyway. I'll be right back."

"Sure," said Jude.

As the officer opened his car door, he called out. "What's the little boy's name."

"Toby," said Jude. "We call him Cowboy Toby."

As the cruiser pulled away, Willy spoke. "You think he's going to bust us?"

"Don't know," said Jude. "But he's going to let us finish what we started."

"He knows we could cut and run," said Ed. "And he knows we won't."

The paint was dry to touch when the officer returned. He approached them carrying a pasteboard box and a small sack.

"The only cake I could find was chocolate with white frosting." He opened the box to reveal a thickly frosted concoction, sure to delight any little boy's heart. "They didn't have anybody who could write his name on it," he said. "So I bought a bottle of chocolate syrup."

"I can do that," Lonesome volunteered. "I can't bake worth a damn, but I'm pretty good at decorating." She was. When she finished, the cake had Toby's name in chocolate script, a cowboy hat, and a pony, all in elegant detail.

The officer took a package of tiny birthday candles from the sack and gave them to Lonesome. "Can't have a birthday cake without candles." He regarded them seriously. "I'm going to the hardware and telling the man I didn't find his paint, but I found some generous people who took up a collection to pay for it."

"We don't have a dime between us," said Jude.

The officer grinned. "I know that. I don't have to tell him the generous person was me."

Jude stood up, surprised at his weak and shaky legs. "Could I have your name. I'd like to pay you back."

"The name's Rico Lopes. I don't want the money back." He started toward his car, stopped, and turned. "Next time I see Shelly, I'm going to tell her she's got some damn good friends."

He saluted as he drove away.

"Let's go deliver Toby's birthday," said Jude.

"Have we got matches for the candles?" asked Lonesome.

"I got Ed's lighter," replied Willy. "If it still works." He took it out, snapped it, and a small flame appeared.

"First thing that's gone right all day," said Ed.

They walked the five blocks light of heart, except for Jude. Even breathing normally hurt, and the exertion made it worse.

He hid his discomfort from his friends. Lonesome, though, watched him carefully.

As they made their way up the short walkway, Ed spoke. "I don't see Shelly's car."

"Probably go to work," said Sherm.

"That's it," said Willy. "The babysitter will be with Toby."

Jude started to knock.

"Wait," said Lonesome. "We've got to light the candles."

When the five candles were lit, Lonesome held the cake in front of her. Sherm passed the bicycle to Jude.

"You give it to him. It's the right way."

Jude held the bike in one hand and knocked. No one answered. He knocked again. Again, no answer.

"Maybe he's next door at the babysitter's apartment," said Lonesome.

"Sure," agreed Willy. "That's got to be it."

Carrying the birthday cake and bike, they trooped across the street to the babysitter's apartment.

Jude knocked. Inside someone stirred, and the lock rattled.

"As soon as you see Toby, start singing Happy Birthday," said Lonesome.

"Don't know the words," Sherm said in panic.

"Just follow the rest of us," Lonesome instructed.

The door opened a crack, and the old woman peered out.

"We've got something for Toby," said Jude.

The old woman opened the door, her expression stricken; she stared at them. "You haven't heard?"

"Heard what?" Jude suddenly felt sick and hollow.

The old woman seemed to have difficulty speaking. "His poor little body just couldn't take any more. He died two hours ago."

Her words sounded to Jude as if they came from inside a great iron bell. His knees buckled, and the world around him closed in; he knew he was falling and didn't care. Blackness overtook him.

CHAPTER FIFTEEN

For a time, Jude thought he was dreaming; faces appeared and drifted away; sometimes familiar faces, but more often, those of strangers.

There were times when he was sure he was dreaming, especially when Jean Marie spoke to him and smiled at him through the mists of time. Even in his dreams, his heart ached, and he tried to turn away, to forget. He wasn't sure when he returned to reality; it came slowly. He lay in a clean, narrow bed, too soft to be comfortable. Thin tubes were taped to his cheeks, and his exploring fingers found a breathing apparatus clipped to his nostrils. A needle in his left arm was connected by clear tubing to a bag hanging from a stand by his bed.

I'm in a hospital, he thought.

He hated hospitals.

The room was small and gray with three other beds, all occupied. Although dim lamps burned, everyone slept, and he assumed it must be night. The smells began to intrude; a harsh alien mix of odors only sickness and the fight against it can generate. The man in the next bed coughed in his sleep.

Why was he in a hospital?

His chest hurt, and his throat felt scratchy and raw, but nothing unbearable. All his extremities were present and seemed to be in working order.

Turning his head, he found a wire terminating in a button pinned to his pillow. If he called a nurse, would she tell him why he was here . . . and when he could leave?

He had to get out of here and get the bicycle to Toby before . . .

The memory returned, and with it, excruciating pain.

During the years of walking the lower path, the path of indifference and apathy, he had built a high, fortress wall to defend himself against this kind of pain. But he found the bulwarks had crumbled to dust, and the pain didn't subside. Staring at the ceiling, trying not to think or feel anything eventually exhausted his already depleted reserves, and the soft edge of sleep eroded his consciousness.

The next time he awoke, sunlight filtered through the window, and sounds came from outside the room. An old man in the next bed began to cough.

A nurse entered the room, a bony, cold-eyed woman with the sharp, impatient movements of a wasp. She gave the old man a pill, gave Jude a disinterested glance, turned on her heel, and stalked out of the room.

Sometime later, a younger woman came in and checked the old man. She turned to Jude.

"You're awake. Good."

"Why am I here?" he asked.

She checked his pulse. "You don't remember?"

"Not much, and it's kind of hazy."

"I'm not surprised. You were unconscious when they brought you in." She stuffed a thermometer in his mouth. "You had pneumonia, but you were already past the crisis." She took the thermometer, read it, and made a note on his chart. Putting her hands on her hips, she studied him. "Still, you had us worried for a few hours."

"Are any of my friends here?"

"No. We finally persuaded them to leave. All four slept in the waiting room until they were sure you were going to be all right." She sighed and shook her head. "And that girl. I had to assure her personally that you would live. I hope you are one hell of a man, because you'd have to be to deserve her."

"She's just a friend," Jude assured her.

The nurse smiled knowingly, and it occurred to him that he had put too much emphasis on the word just.

"How long have I been here?"

"Two days." She checked a gauge attached to the tubes. "Slept most of the time."

"When do I get out?'

She laughed. "I knew that was coming. You'll have to discuss it with your doctor. He'll be here soon. Breakfast is on the way. I suggest you try to eat. It will impress the doctor how well you're doing."

Breakfast arrived, and Jude wasn't absolutely sure what he was eating but was too hungry to care.

The friendly nurse walked into the room, did a double-take, and stopped.

"My God. You finished it all." A concerned look softened her expression. "When was the last time you ate?"

"Don't remember."

"Are you still hungry? I can probably get you another meal."

"I could eat one."

She gave him a look of disbelief. "I seldom see anyone eat even one. Hospital food isn't very good."

"Food is body fuel," said Jude. "Taste is just a bonus."

The second meal didn't taste any better than the first, but he ate it, and when he finished, he felt stronger. The old man coughed some more, and a younger man in the bed by the window complained that the room was too cold. They were both ignored.

Sunlight leaking around the shuttered window grew brighter, and Jude could hear traffic sounds outside. Although he tried, he couldn't altogether avoid thinking about Toby. Six birthdays just didn't seem to be enough. What manner of man would Toby have become, and what accomplishments would be left undone by his loss? Forcing back tears, Jude tried to concentrate on other things. He was grateful when a doctor breezed into the room and grabbed his chart.

"You look a lot better," said the doctor. "Let's check your lungs." He held a cold stethoscope to various places and instructed Jude to breath or cough. Finally, he rolled the stethoscope and dropped it in his smock pocket. Shaking his head somberly, he scribbled something on the chart.

He pulled up a stool and sat by the bed. "The fever is gone and your chest is clear."

"Does that mean I can leave?"

"Not just yet. One more night, and we'll see in the morning. In the meantime, drink a lot of liquids and rest."

"Can you at least take this damn needle out of my arm?"

"That, I can do."

When the doctor left, Jude felt more comfortable but still weary. He resigned himself to a day of boredom, but in fact, he spent a lot of it sleeping. Lunch came and was consumed without enthusiasm. Early evening found him restless and somber.

After supper, he lay listening to the others in the room discuss their ailments, a knee shattered in a car accident, a failing kidney, and a cancerous lung. Closing his eyes, he tried to shut them out.

He heard a shuffling sound and a familiar voice. "Don't look sick."

Opening his eyes, he found Sherm and Ed standing next to his bed. They were both dressed in blue work clothes, new but spattered with dried clumps of concrete.

"Good to see you guys."

He meant it, but the face he'd hoped to see wasn't there.

"You look ornery as ever," said Ed.

With a serious face, Sherm fingered the oxygen tubes. "You breathe okay?"

"The oxygen is just a precaution. The doctor says I'm doing great."

"Are you?" asked Ed.

The question conveyed more than the simple words indicated.

Ed had somehow guessed that Jude was immersed in another crisis; deeper and more threatening than pneumonia.

"I'm coping." Jude flicked a clump of concrete off the sleeve of Sherm's shirt. "Where did you get the new clothes and the concrete?"

Sherm's face lit up. "We got a job."

"You remember Heavy?" asked Ed.

"Sure," said Jude.

"It turns out he's a building contractor, and he needed a couple of guys to help pour foundations."

"Bought us shoes," said Sherm. He lifted his foot to proudly display a new work boot.

"And that's not all," continued Ed. "He's got a big machinery yard with a trailer house on it. Me and Sherm can live there free and watch out for the equipment."

"Not bad for a couple of beach bums," said Jude.

"Yeah," Ed agreed. "Heavy is a good man. He's been down-and-out a few times himself. Says he hired me and Sherm because sane people drive him crazy."

"How's Willy?"

"He wanted to come," said Ed. "But he went home and found his mother was in pretty bad shape. He checked her into a clinic and wants to stay close to her for a while."

"Good for him," said Jude.

Sherm took an envelope from his pocket and handed it to Jude. "From Willy."

He tore open the envelope and inside, found a twenty dollar bill and a note.

Hi friend:

Hope you're feeling better. I won't be able to come down to the beach for a while, but I know you'll understand. I hope the twenty will help out. Money will never replace friendship, but for now it's all I can do.

See you soon,
Wino Willy

Ed picked up a plastic bag and put it on the foot of Jude's bed.

"Lonesome gathered up your best clothes and some other stuff. She said you would be needing them when you get out."

"Where is Lonesome?" asked Jude.

"Don't know," said Sherm.

It took Jude a while to formulate the question.

"I thought she would be with you."

Sherm gave him an odd look and shook his head. "Jude, you pretty smart, sometimes. Sometimes . . . kinda dumb."

Ed looked embarrassed and stuffed his hands in his pockets. "After the doctor convinced her you were going to be okay, she disappeared. Nobody's seen her."

The words struck him like pebbles thrown into a lake. Ripples spread through his mind; little surges of emotion that he couldn't identify.

"When do you get out?" asked Ed.

"Probably tomorrow."

"We come get you," said Sherm.

"But it might not be till late," Ed added. "We got to borrow Heavy's truck."

"Call first," said Jude. "If I get out early, I've got money to take a bus."

"We got to go," said Ed. "You need anything?"

"Nope."

As the two men made their way to the door, Sherm stopped and turned. The big man looked distressed.

"Jude. Lonesome just my best friend." His black eyes were pleading. "She love someone else. You understand?"

A new shadow joined those already filling the dark pit in Jude's heart. Lonesome, in spite of her denial, still loved her ex-husband. "Yes, I guess I do."

That night, Jude slept, but not well. Dreams came where faces mixed and changed, but nothing permanent or recognizable. Toby's face became Jean Marie's, and they both faded, and he could only hear voices. He saw Lonesome walking away from him. When he called, she turned and waved but continued walking. He awoke sweating and shaking.

In the morning, he ate breakfast mechanically and couldn't remember what he'd eaten. A deep gloom gripped his senses, and even the nurses noticed and avoided speaking to him.

The doctor came early and pronounced him fit to leave. In the plastic bag, Jude found his good blue jeans, a T-shirt with no holes, and new pair of inexpensive sneakers. Who had enough money to buy him shoes? When he donned the pants, the pocket jingled, and he found his old knife and a handful of change.

He rode a bus to the city limits of Long Beach, and at the last stop, got out. Standing in the sun, he gratefully soaked in the warmth and light, debating on whether or not to walk the remaining distance. But the bus ride had left him feeling drained, and a five mile walk might be beyond his ability. He compromised and walked slowly along the shoulder, occasionally sticking out his thumb in an attempt to hitch a ride.

As he approached the bridge over the San Gabriel Channel, a delivery truck pulled over. At the wheel sat an old man wearing a shapeless straw hat and a toothless grin.

"Hop in."

Jude climbed up into the seat and collapsed gratefully.

"Where you headed?" asked the old man.

"Sunset Beach."

"Too bad. I was hoping you would want to go all the way to San Clemente." He shifted gears, and the truck lurched back out into traffic. "Got a load of vegetables for a market there. Need someone to help me unload 'em."

"Sorry," said Jude.

"Don't matter. Mostly, I just get tired of driving alone." He glanced at Jude. "You look a little pale. You okay?"

"Just got out of the hospital."

"Nothing too serious, I hope."

"Pneumonia."

"Bad news. That's how I lost Anne. She went in the hospital for a gall bladder operation. Got pneumonia and never came out." He shook his head sadly.

The truck rattled and groaned as he braked for the light at Seal Beach Boulevard. The old man stared ahead. In the distance, Jude could see the causeway over Anaheim Bay.

"Strange thing happened in the back bay couple of days ago," said the old man. "Some damn fool kid in an ocean racer came tearing under the bridge and rammed into a sailboat. Tore the hell outta his boat." The old man turned to Jude. "Maybe you heard about it?"

Jude shook his head.

The light turned green, and the old man pulled away from the intersection.

"Was in the afternoon. A Santa Ana was blowin' and stirring up the water pretty good. The kid was trapped in his boat, and probably would have drowned if some people on shore hadn't rescued him. As luck would have it, a television camera crew was just across the bay shootin' a story on the disappearing wetlands. They filmed the whole thing."

The truck began to labor up the incline onto the causeway, and the old man shifted down.

"Saw the whole damn thing on television that night. Too far away to see faces, but five people, four guys and a gal, risked their necks to save that little fool."

He shook his head in amazement that anyone would rescue a fool.

"They got everybody ashore except the kid driving the boat. He was trapped. A big guy and one wearing a life jacket held the wreck to a buoy while some other fellow went inside the boat to get the driver. The whole damn mess sank on top of him. Even took the big guy and the one in the lifejacket under for a while. Didn't look to me like the one in the life jacket could swim. Didn't stop him though."

"Some people can't be stopped," said Jude

"True," said the old man. "Don't think there's anything that would stop that girl. She was standing on the deck of a navy patrol boat, and when that wrecked boat sank, she hit the water like a cannon ball. God, she was under a long time. When she came up, she had this fellow and the kid by the hair. They sank again, but she just wouldn't let go."

"Sounds like a brave person."

"Damned right she was brave. I bet she is one hell of woman." The old man shook his head. "If I wasn't so cussed old, I'd find her and marry her my own damn self." He downshifted and slowed the truck to avoid a bicyclist riding in the traffic lane. "Course, they was all brave people. When the girl came up holding the last two, she just couldn't stay afloat. By then, the big fellow was on the patrol boat. He grabbed her and hauled all three right up on the deck of the patrol boat, just like yanking a carp out of a mudhole. Never seen anything like it."

"People do strange things," said Jude.

"They sure as hell do. The strangest part is, they just up and disappeared. Nobody knows who the hell they were or where they went. As it turned out, the kid in the ocean racer was the only son of some big land developer that's building himself a mansion in Surfside. He went on television and offered a ten thousand dollar reward to those folks. So far, nobody's collected."

"Maybe they're just not interested in being heroes," said Jude.

"Could be, but that's a pile of money. I'd take it." With one hand, he took off his hat, wiped his brow with his sleeve, and slapped the hat back on his bald head. "Course, that rich fellow is mostly trying to get some of the hero stuff to rub off on him. He don't really care if them people collect or not."

"I expect you're right," said Jude.

The old man laughed. "Some preacher came on television and claimed them people that saved the boy was angels. Said you can't find angels by lookin' for them. You got to need them, and they'll be there. Soon as you don't need 'em any more, they disappear."

"I don't think they're angels," said Jude.

"Oh hell, I don't either. But it does kinda make you think."

The truck rolled slowly into Sunset Beach.

"Where you want me to let you off, son?"

"That little red building up ahead."

"The Shack?" asked the old man. "I've had a beer there now and then."

He pulled in and stopped.

Jude climbed down. "Thanks for the ride."

"Don't mention it." The truck growled away.

Jude stood for a moment, undecided. He could hear noises coming from the Shack; laughter and the jukebox playing too loud. But it was something else that stopped him, that unsettled him.

Sunset Beach had changed.

Physically, every detail was just as it had been a few days before. But now, he felt unconnected, alien, as if this was a world with familiar landmarks but nothing intimate or comfortable. In spite of the warm sun, he shivered.

A light breeze stirred, and a sudden stench filled the air, so powerful that Jude flinched as if he'd been struck a blow.

The breeze stopped, and the odor faded away.

The door to the Shack opened, and Old Dan stepped out, his eyes squinted against the sun. Small and dapper, Old Dan had a face like smooth leather. He always wore a blazer. Today, it was light blue, worn over sharply creased pants of a darker shade. He spied Jude, and his thin lips hinted at a smile.

"Jude, have you got a minute?"

"Time is about all I've got."

Although Jude didn't consider the man a friend or even a close acquaintance, Old Dan was unfailingly polite, if sometimes a bit cold. Idly, Jude wondered why he looked embarrassed.

"I was looking for you," said Dan. "When I got home last week, Dessy told me about you and the girl asking for money. Dessy thought she'd been pretty clever treating you so badly." He put his hands in his pockets and rocked on the balls of his feet. "I had a little talk with her about her attitude."

"Doesn't matter," said Jude.

"It does to me. It's not just you, she's gotten a little too snippity with the customers." He cleared his throat. "But I wasn't really so angry with her as I was with myself."

"You didn't do anything, you weren't even here."

"No. But the question is, would have I done anything if I was here? Would I have given you the money?" He looked down at his shoes. "Sometimes a man's got to be honest with himself, and this is one of those times. I don't think I would have."

"It's history now, Dan."

Old Dan looked up. "Maybe it shouldn't be. When I heard that little boy had died..." Again, he cleared his throat. "It started me thinking. I got a grandson about the same age. I take him to church and try to teach him to be a good man, but I'm not so sure I make a good role model." He gave Jude a thin smile. "This whole thing has left a bad taste in my mouth, real bad. About time I started looking at my priorities."

There didn't seem to be anything to say, so Jude didn't try.

"Well," said Dan. "You are not a priest, and I'm sure you're not interested in my confessions. Why don't you walk with down to the restaurant, and I'll buy you breakfast?"

"Thanks, but they fed me before they let me out of the hospital." Again, the breeze sprang up, this time stronger, and with it came the horrible stench. "What is that smell?"

A wry smile pulled at Dan's thin mouth. "Hal's Bait Shop. Seems his bait freezer has a defrost switch on it, and somehow, it got flipped on. He had about three hundred pounds of squid and a couple hundred pounds of mackerel in there. By the next morning, you could smell them clear into Seal Beach."

Abruptly, the day of the ill-fated mackerel sale came back to Jude, and once again, he saw Willy returning from the back of Hal's Bait Shop with a sly grin on his face. Suddenly, the meaning of Willy's words, There's other ways of dealing with an asshole like Hal, became clear. In spite of his melancholy, he smiled.

Dan straightened his jacket. "If you change your mind about breakfast, stop by the restaurant. I'll tell Dessy to give you whatever you want." He turned and waved as he walked away.

Jude watched a moment before entering the Shack. A young woman Jude remembered vaguely stood behind the bar, rolling dice in a leather cup. Across from her, sat a preppy looking young man in white shorts and a white polo shirt. Jude thought he looked like a carousel pony trying to run with mustangs.

When the dice came to rest, the barmaid squealed with delight and danced a jig. She slapped Preppy on the shoulder. "You have to buy me a drink."

The man shrugged and placed money on the bar. When the girl saw Jude, her eyes went wide.

"Jude, welcome home." She rang up a beer, drew a mug, and took a drink. "Somebody told me you were in the hospital."

"Not anymore. Do you know where I can find Vinny?"

She pouted. "He won't be around for awhile. His ex-wife got real sick, and Vinny's taking care of the kids." She did a little dance and placed her beer on the bar. "Vinny put me in charge till he gets back. You want a beer? It's on the house."

"No thanks," said Jude. "Have you seen Lonesome?"

Another pout, this one touched with anger. "I don't understand what you see in Lonesome. She's taller than you, skinny, and she's hardly got any boobs at all." She shook her ample bosom to demonstrate the lack.

Too tired and blue to respond, he turned and started for the door.

"Oh, don't be mad, Jude. Stay and have a beer."

"Some other time," he said. Outside, the sun had begun to slip into afternoon. Again, the strangeness enveloped him. He drifted down the street without purpose, as if his anchor had slipped, and now, the current carried him away from a once safe harbor.

Without volition, his feet carried him toward Shelly's apartment. Dread tried to slow his steps, but by concentrating, he moved on. At the short pathway to her door, he stopped, relieved to see that the little blue bicycle was gone. The door stood ajar, and he could hear sounds inside. Shelly's old, gray Volkswagen sat in the drive.

Gathering all his courage, he started up the path. At that moment, Shelly stepped outside with a suitcase in her hands. Recognizing Jude, she dropped her burden and ran to him, sweeping him into her arms. She held him so tightly, he could hardly breathe. Stepping back, she peered up into his eyes.

"You were very sick, and I didn't . . ." She took a deep breath. "I just couldn't face another hospital."

"Don't blame you."

"I'm glad you stopped by. Now I can thank you for what you did. And I can apologize for not believing in you."

"No apology—"

"Shush, Jude. I'm trying to be as noble as you and your friends." She gestured toward the suitcase. "Instead, I'm running away."

"I understand," he said. "It helps for awhile, but don't run too long. It gets to be a habit."

For a long time, she stared at him, comprehension dawning in her eyes.

"I should have guessed." Again, she hugged him and stepped back. "Anything I can do for you, Jude?"

"Have you seen Lonesome?"

"I'm sorry, Jude. I haven't. No one has."

He bent and kissed her lightly on the forehead. As he walked away, he looked over his shoulder once. Shelly loaded the suitcase into her car, and keys in hand, slid into the driver's seat.

Turning away, he walked slowly to the beach, down to the wet sand. He remembered the times he'd spent here, lying in the sun without any purpose, other than to be warm. A cool breeze blew in from the sea and ruffled his hair. Even the ocean, the mother of life, seemed distant and elusive. He sat on the sand and stared out at the horizon — blurred by distance and without a boundary.

Somewhere inside him, the force of years of repressed sorrow welled up in an unstoppable geyser. For a decade, he'd held grief inside, enclosed in a crucible of steel; but now, there was simply no vessel that could possibly contain it. Tears streamed down his cheeks, and in a sudden, agonizing eruption, he began to cry. And once the cataract let loose, sorrow and desolation poured out in an uncontrollable flood.

Every inch of his body quaked with anguish; huge, aching sobs wracked his body and tore at the roots of his soul.

How long the tears continued, he wasn't sure, but eventually, his weeping subsided and finally exhausted itself. For a while longer, he sat without moving; his face drenched and his heart barren. When his grief was finally spent, he sensed a presence near him. He looked up.

Lonesome.

Her white shorts and white sleeveless blouse were new, and her hair was brushed till it glowed. She wore no makeup, and a face so full of character and strength needed none. He wondered why he'd never noticed her strength before. She was lovely.

"You look great, Lonesome." The instant her name left his tongue, an important question occurred to him, yet he found himself oddly reluctant to ask. "I don't know your real name."

She smiled and sat on the sand beside him, placing a bottle of wine between them.

"Cassandra. My mother always called me Cassy, and I liked that." She lightly rested her hand on his shoulder. "Do you want me to pretend I didn't see you crying?"

"No."

Gently, she rubbed his shoulder. "This wasn't just for little Toby . . ."

He shook his head, not trusting his voice.

"Will you tell me about it? If you can't, I'll understand."

Clearing his throat, he said. "I can try." He was surprised to find he did want her to know.

With a deep breath, he began. "She was eighteen, we both were. I loved her so much, I hurt when she wasn't near me. And she returned that love. One day, she found a mass on her breast, and within a few days, my world disintegrated."

He stopped, fighting back the lump in his throat that threatened to explode.

"The doctors tried, but nothing worked."

A seagull swooped in and landed gracefully between them and the surf. It regarded Jude a moment, its head cocked to one side. Silently, as if it sensed his distress, it spread its wings and drifted up into the wind.

"How long were you together?" asked Lonesome.

"Less than a year. She wanted to be married, and so did I, and so we were. There were some people who called me a hero and others said I was stupid."

"Stupid?"

"For marrying a dying girl. But I didn't care either way. Nothing could have stopped me."

The tears returned, but gentle tears that rolled slowly down his face.

"In her last days, she was seldom lucid and didn't always know I was there." He stopped and gasped as the old pain stabbed him again. "Moments before she died, she reached up and hugged my neck and spoke her last coherent words. It's all right, Jude. It's all right." He fought to continue. "She waved her hand to me, like a child waving goodbye to her mother . . ."

Lonesome held him against her and stroked his hair.

"And you've been haunted all these years?"

"There must have been something more I could have done."

"I can't imagine what it could have been."

He straightened up and wiped his face.

"There was one doctor with an experimental drug. He said he would consider her as a subject, but it was almost as dangerous as the cancer. I didn't push hard enough."

"You just did your best, Jude, and sometimes, your best is pretty damn good. But none of us are gods, and we don't make godlike decisions." She gripped a handful of his hair gently and turned his face to her. "Can you tell me her name?"

At first, he could not make his voice utter those precious sounds, but something inside him slipped free, and he was able to speak.

"Jean Marie," he said softly. He took a deep breath. "That is the first time I've said her name since she died."

"Yes. I thought it might be."

With a great effort, he pushed away the grief. "You look as if you've made some good decisions."

"Maybe," she smiled. "I called my father. We talked for a long time. He's a tired old man, and he wants his daughter back. He never once mentioned dancing."

"Sounds like a good thing."

"I think so," she said. "Apparently, my mother had set up a trust fund for me I didn't know about. Dad wired me some money, and he's sending the rest as soon as possible. In fact, he wants to bring it in person and visit me a while. It isn't a lot of money, but it's enough for me to get by until I get my California teaching credential." She gave him a cryptic look. "I'm going to be a teacher. And I'm excited about it."

"A teacher," he said. "I can't think of anything better." He sat up and breathed deeply. "When are you leaving?"

"I already have. I rented an apartment in Huntington Beach yesterday. It's kind of empty, but that will change." She looked around as if she was seeing Sunset Beach for the first time. "Things aren't the same here, Jude. I just can't stay."

"I understand."

"Do you, Jude? Do you really understand what I'm trying to tell you?" She turned to face him, and reaching out, placed her fingertips on his lips. "I want to tell you something, but I don't want you to answer me—to speak at all."

"Why?"

"You're a kind man, Jude, and sometimes you let that kindness paint the truth in pretty colors, so it doesn't seem so ugly. I need the truth, even if it's not what I want to hear. Please do this my way."

He nodded. She leaned forward until she was so near, he could feel her breath on his face.

Her voice was as fresh and soft as a breeze among violets.

"I love you, Jude. I have for a very long time."

Jude began to shape his lips to respond. She pressed her fingertips harder.

"No. Don't speak." Her blue eyes held his. "I've loved you, but you were a man in a snow globe. Sometimes you would reach out and touch other people, but you never let anyone reach in and touch you. I'm too proud to beg, so I waited, hoping someday that glass bubble would break. And the other night, when you learned of Toby's death, I think it did.

"I want you, but only if you can give yourself amnesty and love me without reservation. You once told me, that we are all we've got. That is all I want."

She let her fingers trace the line of his cheek. "I'm going to leave you here alone. You need time to think and time to sort your way through the confusion." She took his hand and pressed a slip of paper into it. "This is my new address. If you decide we might make a life together, then you can come to me. Otherwise, it would be better if I never see you again."

She kissed him, lovingly, tenderly, but with a promise of passion that would cause the sea to boil. Rising, she placed the wine bottle near his fingers. For a moment, she hesitated, raised her hand in salute, and walked away.

Until sunset, he didn't move. He wasn't confused, his mind had slipped into an idle state devoid of thought, but rich in emotion.

Darkness came, and the sea spoke soft words, but they were meant for someone else's ear. Through the black sky overhead, celestial dancers wheeled in a stately waltz that had begun long before mankind formed from the dust of exploding stars.

A half moon slipped up from the sea and cast its silver polished light over his new world. And in its strange glow, new thoughts occurred to him, and old ones took on new clarity. He knew what he must do. Rising, he walked along the beach to where a huge, old driftwood stump protruded from the sand.

It had washed ashore long before Jude came here and would be here long after. On the side lit by the moon, he found a clear space that would serve his need.

Using his old pocket knife, he began to carve words into the sodden wood. He worked for hours, carving the letters deep and precise. On the last word, the knife blade snapped, forcing him to finish using the broken remnant. Sunrise came, and he brushed away the last of the shavings. Stepping back, he surveyed his handiwork.

Toby and Jean Marie
Gentle souls that did not abide with us long.

He tossed the broken knife into the sea, picked up the unopened wine bottle, and walked along the beach. Near the street that led to his apartment, he found a young man wrapped in a beach towel asleep among the driftwood logs. An empty wine bottle lay nearby. Carefully, Jude placed the full bottle near the man's fingers and moved on.

His apartment was cool and smelled dank. He looked around, and the alien sense returned. There was nothing to signify the presence of a human soul. Pulling the box from under his bed, he retrieved the red bound volume of Huckleberry Finn. He considered his clothes, but they were little more than rags. With only his book and the clothes he wore, he walked out the door.

Outside, he slipped the scrap of paper from his pocket and memorized Lonesome's — Cassy's — address. Carefully, he refolded it and stuffed it away. The trip to Huntington Beach would take most of the day unless he managed to hitch a ride. He tucked his book under his arm and started down the highway, walking slowly.

The end of his exodus was distant, hidden behind time's gauzy veil, but the journey itself promised excitement and passion and love. And for the first time in a very long time, he knew exactly where he was going.

CHAPTER SIXTEEN

With the death of little Toby, as with the passage of any human spirit, a shadow lingered, one that could never again be filled with light. But it is from the contrast of light and darkness that we perceive our world. In those few days, Jude came to know that a man could not hide himself in the gray world where there is neither bright light nor deep shadow without losing the defining lines of his own soul.

Jude and all his friends, without ever speaking of the concepts, knew that the force that drew them together also gave them the strength to walk separately. Although from that time forward, each one possessed the capacity and resolution to make his own way, the bond between them never weakened and lasted all their lives.

In that brief time of adversity and self-sacrifice, with no one leading and no one following, they had, side by side, walked up and out of the gray world to once again set their feet firmly on the rising path.

FOR FURTHER DISCUSSION

1. How do you think Jude's character changed throughout the book? Do you think he changed for the better or worse?
2. What are your thoughts on the beach bums' character arcs at the end of the book? How did you feel about their personalities before they decided to help Toby?
3. Was there a hero? Who, and why/why not?
4. Has profound grief ever changed the direction of your life?

5. Jude let Jean Marie's death affect his everyday life even years after her passing. Do you think he could have healed from this grief sooner? How and why?
6. The beach bums are often misjudged and are at times suspected as criminals. Why do you think that is? Have you ever been the object of discrimination or prejudice based on your economic status or appearance?
7. Crazy Ed suffered from extreme PTSD. Do you or someone you know have any experience with this disorder? Do you think the author portrayed this well?
8. Do you feel guilt for having missed an opportunity to show another person mercy or empathy?
9. Do you believe poverty is usually the fault of those who are poor or is it simply circumstantial?
10. If you were to make a movie of this book, which actors and actresses would you cast and why?

INSPIRATION FOR
SUNSET TOMORROW

Sunset Tomorrow is based in the real-life community Sunset Beach, a small beach town just south of Long Beach, California.

The story is set in the late 1960s, during the middle years of the Vietnam War. Ervin believes this was the best of times for Sunset Beach. In those years, it had a great measure of heart and character. It is a different place now, and he wanted to set his tale in the era before it became too civilized.

All of the characters in *Sunset Tomorrow* are fictitious, except for Jude. The arc of Jude's character is based on the author's own life. Ervin mirrored his own flaws and virtues to create Jude's personality and beliefs. Many of the incidents that occur throughout this story were inspired by real events from Ervin's life, changed both in order and outcome.

ABOUT THE AUTHOR

E. Ervin Tibbs was born into a family of migrant farm workers, camped under a fig tree in central California. It was 1939, the tail end of the Great Depression, and many still suffered its aftermath. In Europe, the dogs of war were straining at their leashes, but in the U.S. penny candy actually cost a penny. Throughout his lifetime, Ervin has survived by being flexible. He has picked cotton, built boats, worked as a roustabout, served a hitch in U.S. Army

Intelligence, and the list could go on much longer. Ervin's writing has been nominated for many awards. His short story *Winter Falcon* was the runner-up in the 1992 St. Martin's Press Best New Detective contest. Another of his short stories, *The Shaman's Apprentice*, was a finalist in the 2002 Time Warner Best Fantasy Contest. He is now a retired chemist and spends his days building custom guitars and writing.

More from CamCat Publishing

An Excerpt from
A Grave Too Many by William Norris

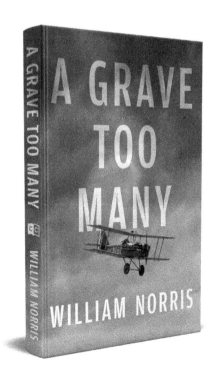

Chapter One

The shadow of the ancient biplane danced and fluttered over Salisbury Plain. Etched sharp by the bright May sunshine, the SE5a ran on toward the village, growing larger as it descended in a graceful turn toward the grass landing strip. The young pilot scanned the ground from the open cockpit. He watched the racing shadow flick across thatched roofs and rambling gardens, touching the village graveyard with a passing shroud and moving swiftly on. On a bench beside the tombstones, he could see, quite clearly, the upturned face of a tiny seated figure. The figure waved.

Beneath his goggles, the pilot grinned and raised a gloved hand to return the salute before concentrating once more on his approach and landing. It would not do to bend it; this was the only one left. The very last genuine SE5a in the whole damn world, outside of a museum.

He lined up the blunt engine cowling with the runway markers and moved the throttle quadrant until the roar of the Hispano-Suiza engine subsided to a gentle burble. The nose of the SE5a sank into a long, gliding approach and the ground rose up to meet it. Now, a steady pull on the cord-bound ring of the joystick, and the rate of descent eased. He shifted his gaze to the side as the long cowling rose to cut his forward vision, and watched the blades of grass racing by beneath the trailing edges of the lower wings.

The noise of the wind in the wires died away, the stick was back in his belly, and he felt a small jar through the airframe as the tail skid touched fractionally before the main wheels. There were no brakes. The SE5a bumped along gently for fifty yards and rolled to a halt. He gave it a small burst of throttle, turned, and taxied slowly toward the hangar.

"She's fine," he told the waiting mechanic. "Just fine." He gave the side of the cockpit an affectionate pat and walked away slowly with real regret. They did not make them like that anymore, and it was a pity. That was the end of true flying for a month, until they let him take the old warplane up again on the next public-display day. Tomorrow he would be back in the draftless efficiency of a Boeing 747, hauling tourists and businessmen on the long flight to New York. It was a living, but that was all.

The pilot left his helmet on, the goggles pushed up on his forehead, as he wandered through the ice-cream-licking crowds to the 1946 MG sports car that was his second love. Truth to tell, he rather enjoyed the Red Baron image. He caught the admiring glances of several attractive girls and flicked the silk scarf back around his neck. Then, clambering into the vestigial cockpit of the MG, he nudged it into life and set off down the hill. There was one more thing he wanted to do before he left Upavon that day.

The old man had been dreaming. It was a familiar dream, and he savored it with a smile as he dozed on the green bench beside the upright sentinels of the grave markers. The graves around him were mostly of airmen — relics of the days long ago when Upavon had been an operational airfield in two world wars. Perhaps, he often thought, that was the reason the dream came most vividly when he sat on this bench. He had not slept long — only closing his eyes when the SE5a sank behind the trees on the ridge across the valley — but the dream had carried him back more than sixty years, to the days of his youth and a muddy field close to the Allied lines on the western front.

It was 1917, a fine September morning, and the noise of the guns in the distance was almost drowned out by birdsong. Outside the makeshift hangars in a field on the outskirts of Flez, a line of SE5a's had just returned from dawn patrol. Mechanics fussed around them as a truck deposited the trio of replacement pilots outside the tent that served as squadron headquarters.

The war was at its height and not going well. The French army had mutinied, and in the mud and devastation of the Ypres Salient, more than a half million men were dying in the bitter struggle for a place called Passchendaele.

None of it seemed to matter as he stood there in his high-buttoned tunic with shining Royal Flying Corps wings on the left breast. Seven months before, he had been an engineering student at Cape Town University who had never even seen an airplane. Now he was an operational fighter pilot.

"Hey, Shorty!" The reverie within a dream was interrupted. A young man in a leather flying jacket was calling to him from the flight line. "Do you think you can fly one of these things? I reckon you won't see out of the cockpit."

The newcomer rummaged in the top of his kit bag and produced a pair of leather-covered cushions, brandishing them at the other pilot. "No problem," he shouted back. Jibes about his lack of height had once upset him, but now he had ceased to care. If God had meant him to grow taller than five foot two, God would doubtless have done something about it. God had made him a fighter pilot. That was what mattered.

The dream skipped in time, and now he was in the air, screaming down out of the sun at full throttle toward the unsuspecting Rumpler two-seater that was climbing for height far below him. Too late, the enemy pilot realized his danger and began to turn away. But the twin Vickers machine guns were cocked and ready, and he saw the German observer crumple as he poured the first burst into the rear cockpit.

A wild cavorting in the sky, two more bursts, and the Rumpler was falling like a bird with a broken wing. He saw it crash into a field beside the silver thread of the river Somme and burst into flames.

The old man stirred awake. His cheeks were wet for the thought of the men he had killed. So many men. Fifty-four victories, they said, but those were only the kills that could be confirmed. And all in those thirteen savage months before the Armistice brought the madness to a close. So many men. So many widows.

He opened his eyes slowly, feeling cheated. The dream had ended before its usual climax: the scene he cherished most, where he stood in the long room at Buckingham Palace, and the bearded, long-dead king pinned the medals on his chest.

The Victoria Cross, the Distinguished Service Order, the Military Cross and the Distinguished Flying Cross. More medals than any South African had ever won. Medals to mark his achievement as the fifth-ranking ace in the whole of the Allied air force. Medals he had not seen for years, tucked away in a secret drawer in the back of his writing bureau.

The voice that woke him had a familiar inflection. It startled him.

"Sir, forgive me, but I've been wanting to meet you for months."

The voice was out of his boyhood—the flat nasal drawl of the highveld. But its owner . . .

Dear God, thought the old man, I must have died in my sleep, or else I am dreaming still. The flying helmet, the goggles, the silk scarf and leather jacket . . . it's Harry van der Merwe, my old wingman from Eighty-Four Squadron.

But van der Merwe was dead, long dead. He had flown out to meet Baron Manfred von Richthofen's circus in the cold light of dawn and had never returned. The old man closed his eyes again and opened them slowly. The apparition was still there. He struggled stiffly to his feet. Age had diminished him further, and he stood no taller than the pilot's chest.

"Who . . . who are you?" There was no sign of a South African accent in his own voice. That had long since gone.

"Sir, my name is John Kruger. I'm the pilot of that SE5a you waved to a short time ago. I've seen you here, on the same spot, every time I fly over. You always wave, and I always wave back. I thought it was time we got acquainted. I was just curious, I guess," he added lamely. A wary look, almost hostile, had come into the old man's eyes.

"You're not English," the old man challenged.

"No, sir. As a matter of fact I come from South Africa."

"Go away," the old man said. "Leave me alone. I'm English, damn you. This is my country. We don't want any bloody Boers over here. Be off with you."

He raised his stick. The pilot stepped back quickly.

"But sir, I only thought, because you seemed so interested in the plane —"

"Young man, I have no interest in aeroplanes, and I have never waved to one in my life. I come here sometimes for peace and quiet. That is all." He gestured toward the gravestones beside the graveled path. "I want to be left in peace with my friends."

Kruger's eyes followed the movement, taking in the neat rows of uniform headstones and the well-kept lawn. Suddenly he froze. "That's odd," he said. "This grave over here. I've never been to this cemetery, but I could swear that I've seen that name before." He shook his head in puzzlement and moved closer to one stone standing in the center of a row of three. The old man remained perfectly still, save for the pulse of a swollen vein beating in his temple.

Kruger read the headstone aloud. "Flight Lieutenant Andrew Weatherby Beauchamp-Proctor VC, DSO, MC, DFC. Killed at Upavon, June 21, 1921." Beneath the inscription was a replica of the Victoria Cross, and the inscription "For Valour."

He straightened up, his voice excited. "But I know this guy. At least, I know of him. He was the local hero back in my hometown, Mafeking. When we were at school we all learned about Andrew Proctor and the way he won the VC. Why, he used to fly SE5a's, too. Perhaps that's why I got mixed up in this business. But . . . " Kruger paused, his brow furrowed. "He can't be buried here. I mean, he's buried back home in Mafeking. I know he is. I've seen the grave. I . . . I don't understand."

He turned to look at the old man, but found he was talking to himself. Through the gates of the cemetery, fifty yards away, the small black figure of the man was hurrying away down the hill, coat flapping, as though the devil himself were in pursuit.

Kruger stood by the grave of Andrew Beauchamp-Proctor for several minutes, deep in thought. "Queer," he murmured. "Very queer. Whoever heard of a man being buried in two places at once?"

He walked slowly back to his car and drove away along the winding Wiltshire lanes.

CamCat Books

VISIT US ONLINE FOR
MORE BOOKS TO LIVE IN:
CAMCATBOOKS.COM

FOLLOW US

CamCatBooks   @CamCatBooks   @CamCat_Books

CPSIA information can be obtained
at www.ICGtesting.com
Printed in the USA
LVHW012243130121
676362LV00006B/1231